LANG | MUTTI | SZYMANOWICZ | MARTINBROUGH

MEYER

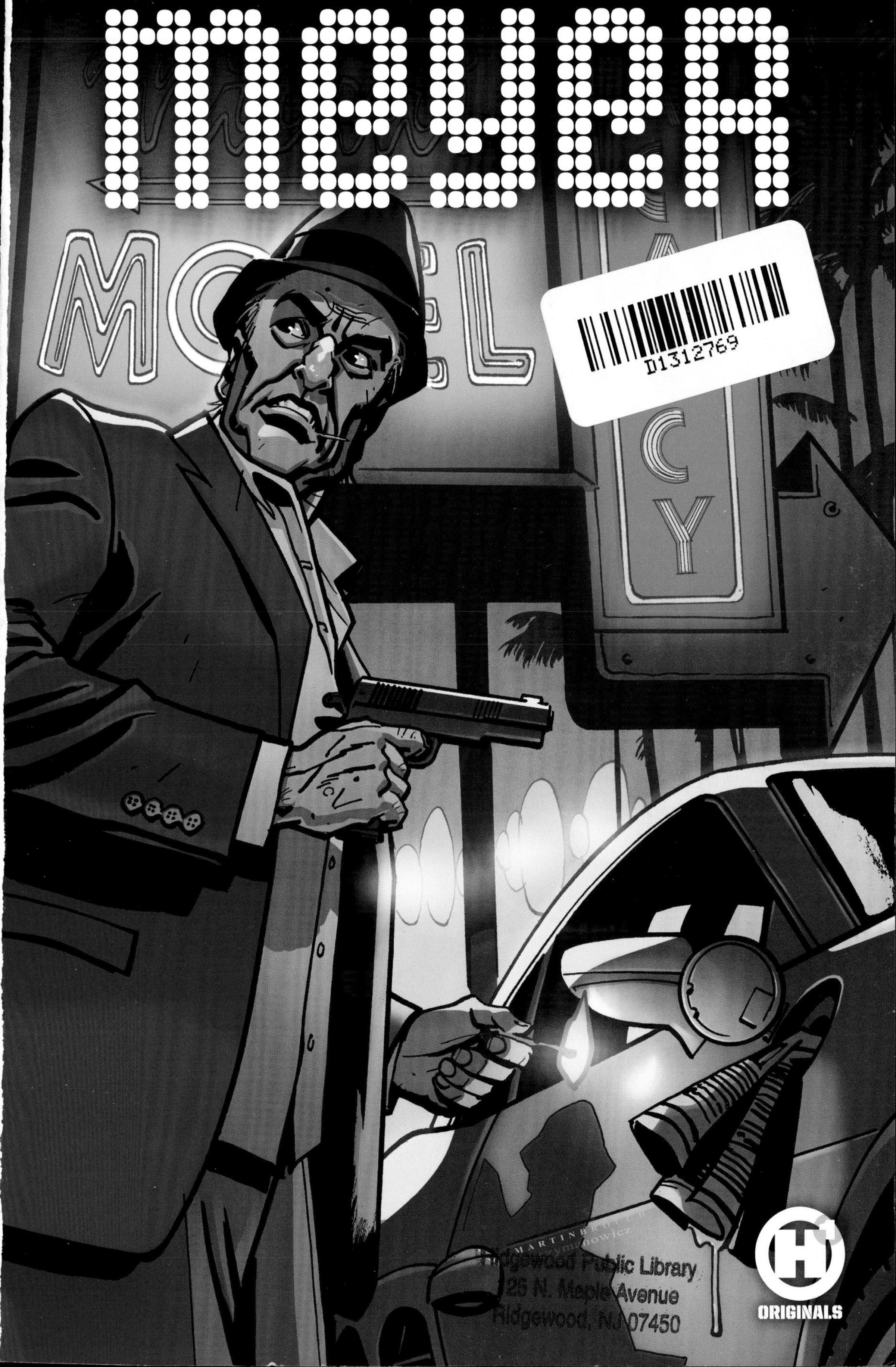

ORIGINALS

GRAPHIC FIC
LANG

WRITER | **JONATHAN LANG**
ARTIST | **ANDREA MUTTI**
COVER | **SHAWN MARTINBROUGH**
COLOR ARTIST | **ANDRE SZYMANOWICZ**
LETTERS | **A LARGER WORLD STUDIOS**

DIRECTOR OF CREATIVE DEVELOPMENT | **MARK WAID**
CHIEF CREATIVE OFFICER | **JOHN CASSADAY**
SENIOR EDITOR | **FABRICE SAPOLSKY**
ASSISTANT EDITOR | **AMANDA LUCIDO**
LOGO DESIGN | **RIAN HUGHES**
SENIOR ART DIRECTOR | **JERRY FRISSEN**

CEO AND PUBLISHER | **FABRICE GIGER**
COO | **ALEX DONOGHUE**
CFO | **GUILLAUME NOUGARET**
DIRECTOR OF SALES AND MARKETING | **AILEN LUJO**
SALES AND MARKETING ASSISTANT | **ANDREA TORRES**
SALES REPRESENTATIVE | **HARLEY SALBACKA**
PRODUCTION COORDINATOR | **ALISA TRAGER**
DIRECTOR, LICENSING | **EDMOND LEE**
CTO | **BRUNO BARBERI**
RIGHTS AND LICENSING | **LICENSING@HUMANOIDS.COM**
PRESS AND SOCIAL MEDIA | **PR@HUMANOIDS.COM**

SPECIAL THANKS FROM JONATHAN LANG:
Thank you to my incredible wife, Sara Sellar, my mentor, Dean Haspiel,
my creative compadre, Michael Lapinski, my parents, Drs. Arnold and Gale
Lang, my siblings, David and Samantha, editorial insights, Stephen Christy
and Rebecca Taylor, inspiration, The Coen Bros., Billy Corben, Michael Chabon,
Ed Brubaker, and Charles Willeford.

Dedicated to my grandfathers, Phillip Mitnick, a real Brooklyn wiseguy,
Herschel Lang, a true talmudic wise man, and my gift of a son, Henry Asher
Lang, who gives me wisdom each day.

SPECIAL THANKS FROM ANDREA MUTTI:
To my old uncle Enio.

MEYER. This title is a publication of Humanoids, Inc. 8033 Sunset Blvd. #628,
Los Angeles, CA 90046. Copyright © 2019 Humanoids, Inc., Los Angeles (USA).
All rights reserved. Humanoids and its logos are ® and © 2019 Humanoids, Inc.
Library of Congress Control Number: 2019940052

H1 is an imprint of Humanoids, Inc.

No portion of this book may be reproduced by any means without the express
written consent of the copyright holder except for artwork used for review
purposes. Printed in Spain.

1.

*"When you look
to the heights,
Hold on to your hat."*

– Yiddish Proverb

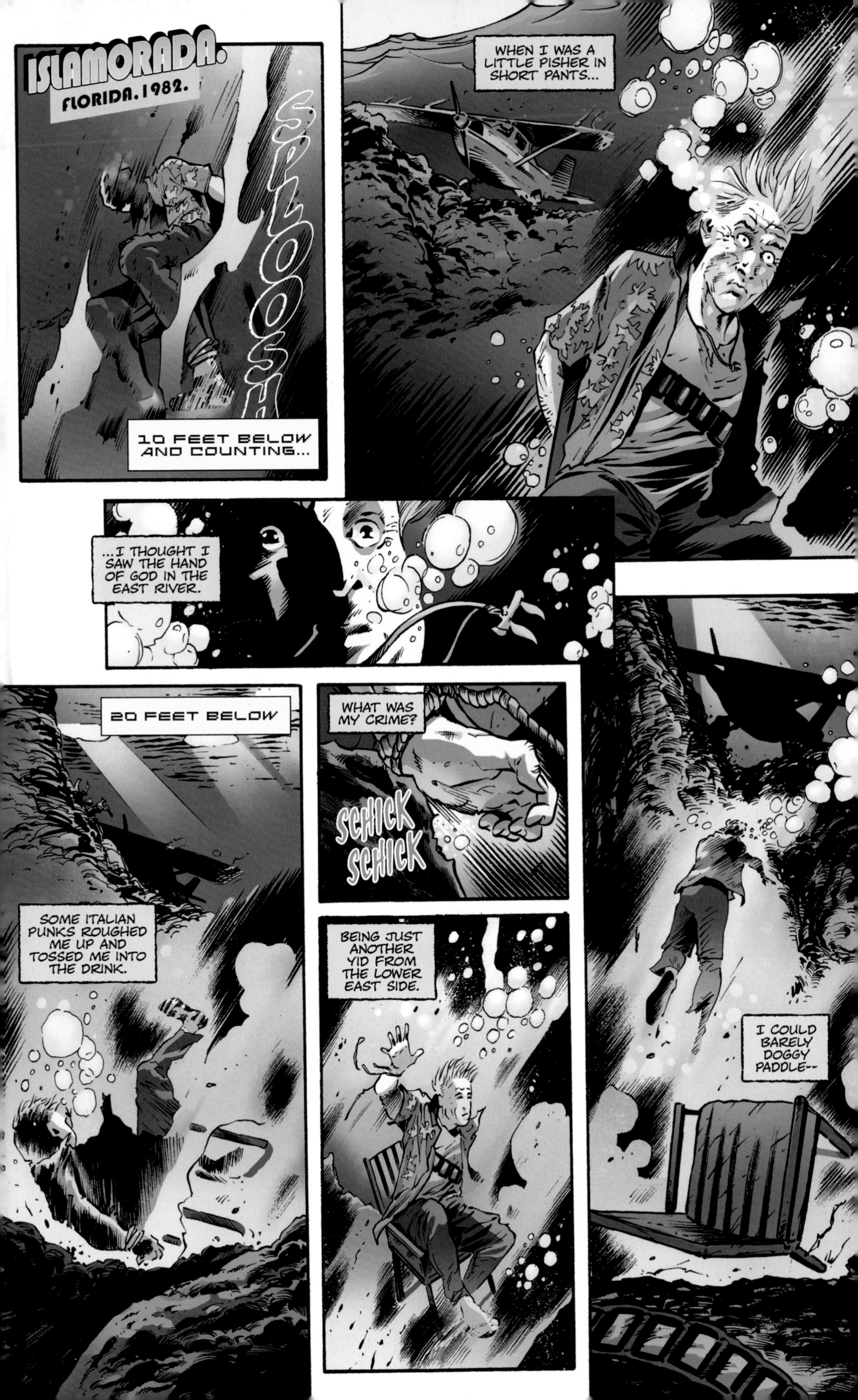
ISLAMORADA.
FLORIDA. 1982.
SPLOOOSH
10 FEET BELOW AND COUNTING...
WHEN I WAS A LITTLE PISHER IN SHORT PANTS...
...I THOUGHT I SAW THE HAND OF GOD IN THE EAST RIVER.
20 FEET BELOW
SOME ITALIAN PUNKS ROUGHED ME UP AND TOSSED ME INTO THE DRINK.
WHAT WAS MY CRIME?
SCHICK SCHICK
BEING JUST ANOTHER YID FROM THE LOWER EAST SIDE.
I COULD BARELY DOGGY PADDLE--

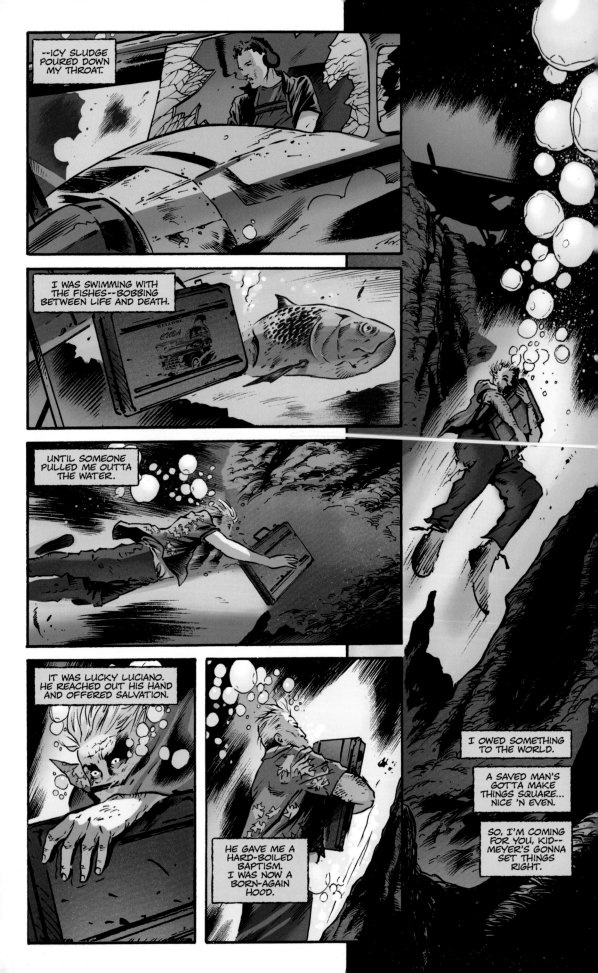

--ICY SLUDGE POURED DOWN MY THROAT.

I WAS SWIMMING WITH THE FISHES--BOBBING BETWEEN LIFE AND DEATH.

UNTIL SOMEONE PULLED ME OUTTA THE WATER.

IT WAS LUCKY LUCIANO. HE REACHED OUT HIS HAND AND OFFERED SALVATION.

HE GAVE ME A HARD-BOILED BAPTISM. I WAS NOW A BORN-AGAIN HOOD.

I OWED SOMETHING TO THE WORLD.

A SAVED MAN'S GOTTA MAKE THINGS SQUARE... NICE 'N EVEN.

SO, I'M COMING FOR YOU, KID-- MEYER'S GONNA SET THINGS RIGHT.

MIAMI.

SHADYBROOKE RETIREMENT HOME. TWO DAYS AGO.

PERIPHERAL ARTERY DISEASE IS NO JOKE. YOU NEED TO EXERCISE TO IMPROVE YOUR CIRCULATION.

GET INTO THE WATER, MORRIS.

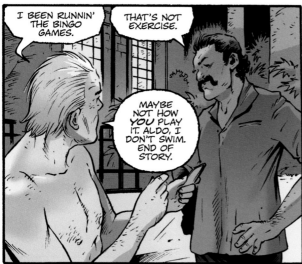

I BEEN RUNNIN' THE BINGO GAMES.

THAT'S NOT EXERCISE.

MAYBE NOT HOW *YOU* PLAY IT. ALDO, I DON'T SWIM. END OF STORY.

DON'T TEST YOUR LUCK.

YOU'RE NOT GOING TO LIKE IT WHEN YOU GET GANGRENE.

GANGRENE?

COMES ON QUICK. WOULDN'T SURPRISE ME IF A DOCTOR HAD TO AMPUTATE IN A FEW DAYS.

IF A SAWBONES WANTS A PIECE OF ME--TELL HIM TO TAKE A NUMBER.

CRACKLE
CRACKLE

THE ELEPHANT GRAVEYARD... IT IS THERE, ACCORDING TO LEGEND, OLDER ELEPHANTS INSTINCTIVELY DIRECT THEM-SELVES WHEN THEY REACH A CERTAIN AGE.

THEY THEN DIE THERE...

ALONE-- FAR FROM THE GROUP.

OY VEY.

SPLOOSH

THIS SUCKS.

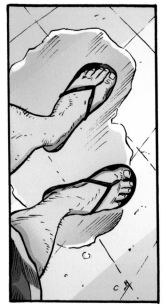

HEY, OLD MAN!

YOU'RE SUPPOSED TO DRY OFF AFTER POOL USE. THOSE ARE THE RULES!

HEH, RULES?

STICK TO THE RULES AND YOU'LL BE MOPPING FLOORS THE REST OF YOUR LIFE.

MY MOTHER CLEANS FLOORS... IT'S HONEST WORK!

...AND THEY'RE IN THE FINAL STRETCH!

NOT IN THE CARDS FOR YOU TODAY, LEGS.

LUCK CAN BE A REAL BITCH.

MILENA...?

RIIIP

YOU NEVER GAVE ME THE FULL TOUR. YOUR OFFICE, NOW!

RIIIPRIIIP
RIIIP

LEGS, I DON'T LIKE ABUSING THE ELDERLY. NOT THE WAY US COLOMBIANS ARE RAISED. RESPECT FIRST.

SMAAASH

WE HAD A DEAL, MILENA. I'M A MAN OF MY WORD.

VERY PRETTY WORDS. WHERE *THE HELL* IS MY COCAINE?!

MY PILOT, NICKY TUESDAY, HE KNOWS. HE KNOWS WHERE THE GOODS ARE. YOU FIND HIM, YOU'LL FIND WHAT'S YOURS.

I DON'T NEED TO FIND HIM, I FOUND YOU.

WHERE IS THAT PLANE?!

SLAP

I KNOW THAT SOMETIMES YOU OLD PEOPLE GET SOME PROBLEMS WITH YOUR MEMORY. YOU LEAVE THE HOUSE, WANDER AROUND, WONDER HOW THE HELL YOU GOT SOMEWHERE.

BLAAAAM

YOU JUST SIT DOWN IN THAT CHAIR AND HAVE A GOOD THINK. WHEN YOU REMEMBER WHERE NICKY TUESDAY IS, YOU CALL ME.

¿COMPRENDÉ?

NNN... NNNGHH...

THANKS, MR. FEINSTEIN, YOU REALLY DID ME A SOLID.

THERE'S A TIME IN A MAN'S LIFE WHERE, FOR A GLIMMER, HE HAS CONTROL. IT MIGHT NOT BE VERY MUCH, BUT HE KNOWS WHAT'S HIS.

HE REALIZES THAT ONLY THIS TIME EXISTS. THERE'S NUTHIN' HE CAN DO TO GET IT BACK.

HE CAN LOOK AT PHOTOS. HE CAN TELL STORIES...

HELL, HE CAN GET THE SAME PEOPLE BACK TOGETHER IN A ROOM, BUT THAT GLIMMER IS ABSOLUTE BLACKNESS.

IT HAS NO SHAPE.

DAMMIT, LEGS-- WHERE THE HELL ARE YA?

TO PUT WORDS AROUND IT ONLY MAKES IT FURTHER AWAY-- LESS REAL.

TO SPEAK OF IT IS MURDER.

LEGS-- IT'S ME. ANY WORD ON *THE LAZY PELICAN?* I NEED MY PAPERS. IT'S BEEN THREE MONTHS.

THEY'RE GONNA CUT MY FOOT OFF!

MEYER, I CAN'T TALK TO YOU. I GOT MY OWN PODIATRY TROUBLES.

IT'S NOT JUST FEDS CONNECTING THE DOTS ANYMORE. IF YOU'RE SMART, YOU'LL STAY HIDDEN.

CLICK

I GOTTA SKEDADDLE OUTTA HERE *TODAY.*

BIZ SHPETER.

*YIDDISH: SEE YOU LATER

NEXT YEAR IN JERUSALEM.

RATTLE RATTLE

MR. COHEN?
MR. COHEN?

DOESN'T MATTER WHAT MY P.O. SAYS--

--I JUST MIGHT BE IN THE RIGHT PLACE AFTER ALL.

HUH.

I SEE WE GOT OURSELVES A HOODLUM HERE.

WHATEVER, POPS.

MORRIS! WHERE ARE YOU GOING?

I WANNA WATCH THE SUNSET AND TAKE IN THE OCEAN BREEZE. WHAT'S IT TO YOU?

YOU KNOW ONLY FAMILY CAN SIGN YOU OUT. ARE YOU FEELING ALRIGHT, MORRIS?

NOT ASKING THE RIGHT QUESTION, ALDO. WHAT YOU SHOULD BE ASKING IS--WHAT CAN I DO FOR YOU?

COUPLE OF SWIGS OF THAT--AND IT'S LIKE BEING A TEENAGER AGAIN, BACK ON THE BEACHES OF HAVANA.

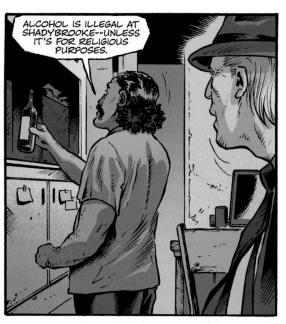

ALCOHOL IS ILLEGAL AT SHADYBROOKE--UNLESS IT'S FOR RELIGIOUS PURPOSES.

PROHIBITION'S OVER I CAN BUY GREAT CUBAN RUM DOWN ON CALLE OCHO.

I'VE SIPPED MOJITOS WITH BAUTISTA AND YOU'RE GONNA GIVE *ME* THE HIGH HAT?

BOY, YOU GOT SOME IMAGINATION, MORRIS.

DAVID, ESCORT MR. GLUCK BACK TO HIS ROOM.

YOU'RE GONNA LEAVE ME WITH THIS GONIF?*

LET'S GO, MR. GLUCK.

*THIEF

WANNA PINCH ME?

GO AHEAD, SNAG SOME BRACELETS.

SHALOM, MR. COHEN. YOU WERE ONE'A THE GOOD ONES.

THE WESTERN WALL, HUH? HAVE YOU BEEN TO ISRAEL?

YOU KNOW, I'M A JEWBAN... A JEWISH CUBAN.

MAZEL TOV TO YOU.

I WAS TRYING TO BE *NICE*. THINK I WANNA TALK TO SOME OLD MAN ALL DAY?

I'M ONLY DOING THIS FOR COMMUNITY SERVICE, Y'KNOW.

COMMUNITY SERVICE, MY ELBOW. YOU GOT A PROBATION OFFICER, DON'T YA?

WHAT? NO--YOU DON'T KNOW WHAT YOU'RE TALKING ABOUT.

IT'S ALL RIGHT, KID. EVERYONE GETS PINCHED SOONER OR LATER.

I GOT IT ALL MAPPED OUT. IT'S A STRAIGHT SHOT RIGHT OUTTA LOSERVILLE. YOU GOT A CAN?

YOU KNOW-- A CAR? FOUR WHEELS?

YOU KIDDIN'? YOU'RE TALKING TO THE OWNER OF THE RADDEST FIREBIRD IN DADE COUNTY.

HOW'D YOU LIKE TO BE MY WHEELMAN?

MAYBE SOME KESEV* WILL EXPLAIN BETTER THAN I CAN.

*MONEY

HOW MUCH IS THERE? WHERE'D YOU GET THIS? WHO *ARE* YOU?

QUIT GIVING ME THE THIRD DEGREE. YOU HELP ME ANKLE THIS JUG, I GOT PLENTY OF ANSWERS AND MORE SCRATCH TO BOOT.

SHOW UP TONIGHT AFTER HOURS. PARK IN THE BACK, AND WE'RE OFF. *FARSHTEYN?*

SO-- DO WE GOT A DEAL?

I CAN'T HELP YOU, MORRIS.

IT'LL BREAK MY MOM'S HEART.

I KNOW YOU'RE NO BOY SCOUT. I SAW YOUR ITCHY LITTLE FINGERS BACK IN MR. COHEN'S ROOM.

LIGHTS OUT, MORRIS.

CLICK

MIAMI.
OAKDALE APARTMENTS.

♪ MY MOTHER WAS A TAILOR
SHE SEWED MY NEW
BLUE JEANS ♪
MY FATHER WAS A GAMBLIN' MAN
DOWN IN NEW ORLEANS
CLICK

STORY OF
MY LIFE.

I'M A VERY GENEROUS MAN,
MRS. GREENE. I'VE GIVEN YOUR
NO-GOOD SON A FREE PARKING SPOT
FOR CHRIST'S SAKE. BUT THREE
MONTHS' RENT...INEXCUSABLE.

THE GREENES
LANG
SAPOLSKY

DON'T SAY A WORD
ABOUT MY BOY DAVID.
HE GREW UP WITHOUT
A FATHER

WE ALL GOT OUR TROUBLES,
MRS. GREENE. I'LL KEEP IT SIMPLE.
YOU COME UP WITH THAT MONEY BY NEXT
WEEK OR YOU'RE GONE. UNDERSTOOD?

BACK OFF! YOU GOT A
PROBLEM, TAKE IT UP
WITH ME. I'M THE MAN
OF THE HOUSE.

SOME MAN OF
THE HOUSE. YOU GOT
YOUR MOTHER FIRED.
HAVE A GOOD EVENING,
MRS. GREENE.

MAMA,
WHAT'S HE
TALKING
ABOUT?

THE KIDS
AT RANSOM
HIGH HAVE
BEEN TALKING
ABOUT YOUR
ARREST.

THE
ADMINISTRATION--
THEY DON'T WANT
ANY TROUBLE.

I BEEN SCRUBBING FLOORS THERE SINCE YOU WERE IN KINDERGARTEN SO YOU COULD GET INTO THAT SCHOOL.

EVER ASK *ME* HOW THAT FELT? YOU COULD'VE WORKED ANYWHERE.

WHO'S GONNA HIRE A CUBAN IMMIGRANT WITH NO EDUCATION, HUH? THEY THINK WE'RE *MARIELITOS*-- CRIMINALS.

AND YOU GOTTA PROVE THEM RIGHT.

YOU DON'T UNDERSTAND. EVERYONE FROM MY CLASS WENT OFF TO COLLEGE!

I'M STUCK WITH YOU AS A ROOMMATE AND A MOP IN MY HAND! WHAT DO I GOT?

THAT'S *YOUR FAULT*, NOT MINE. YOU GOT LOVE... DIGNITY. THAT SHOULD BE ENOUGH.

In order to take, one must first give.

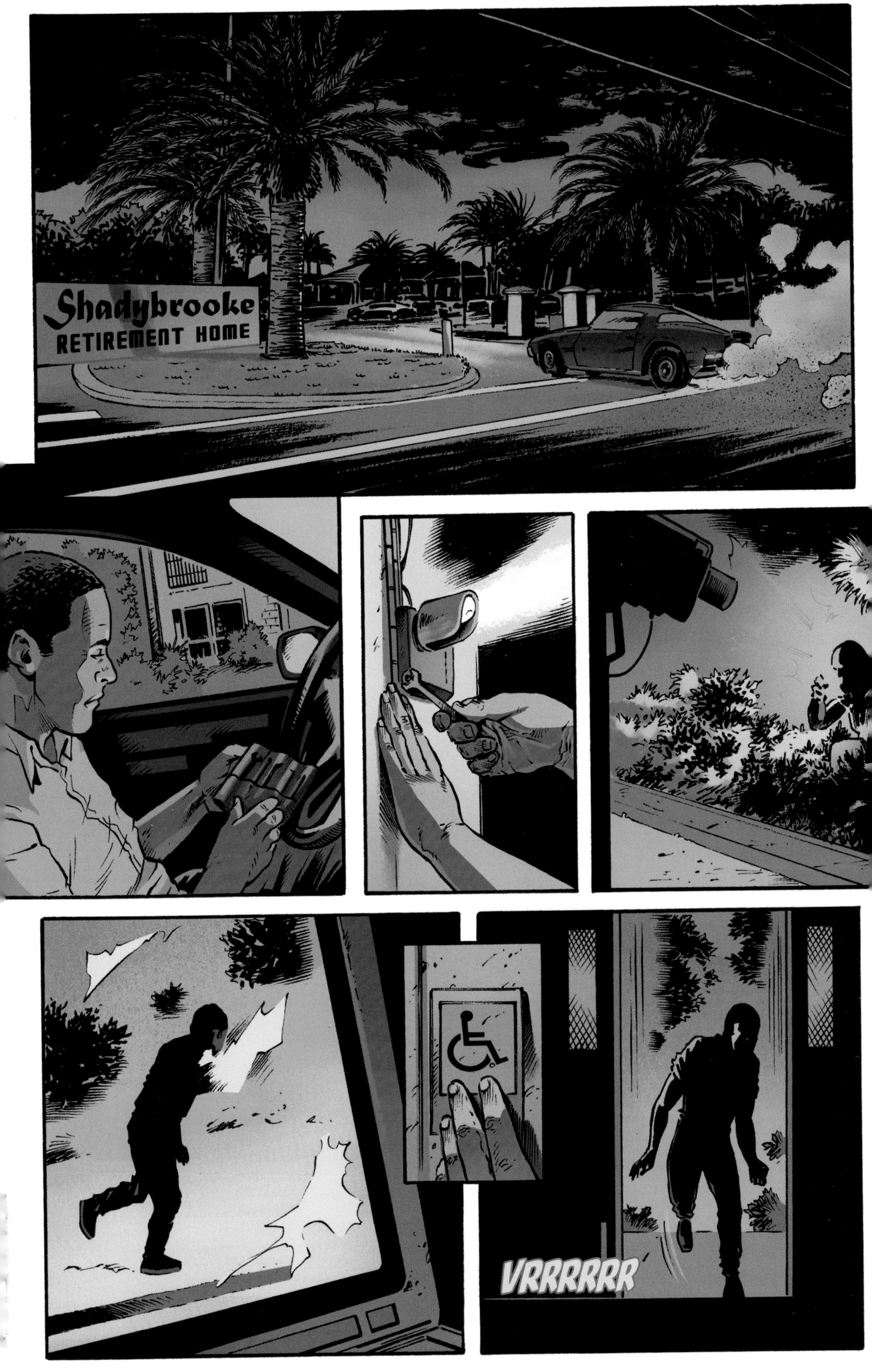
Shadybrooke
RETIREMENT HOME
VRRRRRR

HEY, MORRIS!

DAMMIT, KID! YOU DON'T SNEAK UP ON ALTER COCKERS.

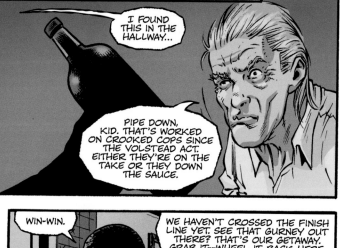

I FOUND THIS IN THE HALLWAY...

PIPE DOWN, KID. THAT'S WORKED ON CROOKED COPS SINCE THE VOLSTEAD ACT. EITHER THEY'RE ON THE TAKE OR THEY DOWN THE SAUCE.

WIN-WIN.

WE HAVEN'T CROSSED THE FINISH LINE YET. SEE THAT GURNEY OUT THERE? THAT'S OUR GETAWAY. GRAB IT--WHEEL IT BACK HERE.

BUT MY CAR'S RIGHT OUTSIDE. WHY DO WE NEED A GURNEY?

STOP CRACKING WISE AND GRAB THE GURNEY, *FARSHTAY?*

WHAT'S THAT MEAN?

IT'S YIDDISH--MEANS "UNDERSTAND."

LIKE *CAPISCE?*

POP

THAT'S FOR ITALIANS, WISEGUY. NOW, GET GOING.

A LITTLE INSURANCE NEVER HURTS.

HIT THE GAS, KID--

--THEY'RE SWAPPING OUT GOONS.

SMAAACK

LET'S MAKE TRACKS!

WHAT'S THE SHOWER GRAB BAR FOR?

TO HELP US GIVE 'EM THE SLIP!

VUUUCK

KLLNNNG

ZAY GEZUNT*, YA TWITS. IT'S BEEN A HELLUVA ROMP.

*BE WELL/FAREWELL

CRAAACK

WHO THE HELL *ARE* YOU?

KEEPING *THAT* UNDER MY HAT 'TIL YOU GET ME TO THE PONIES.

YOU WANT ANSWERS, KID--STEP ON IT!

2.

"When a thief kisses you, count your teeth."

– Yiddish Proverb

ISLAMORADA.
THE HUNGRY TARPON.
YESTERDAY.

FWIIIIIIISSSSH

THE HUNGRY TARPON

I DON'T DRINK CAFÉ CUBANO 'CAUSE I AIN'T NO MARICON.

THE BLACK STUFF FROM THE GASOLINERA--

--THAT REVS ME UP REAL GOOD. BUT I BEEN THINKIN' ABOUT WHAT YOU SAID, RAFA, ABOUT THE HEAT MAKING YOU ESTUPIDO.

YOU WERE RIGHT ABOUT THAT.

MAMA

THE BODY NEEDS GLUCOSE FOR ENERGY TO REGULATE.

TO KEEP YOU COOL.

SO I WAS SITTIN' IN MY CAR SWEATIN' MY CAJONES OFF, JUST WAITIN' TO CAP SOMEONE 'N I THOUGHT, I COULD BE MAKIN' BAD DECISIONS.

MAYBE MY BRAIN DON'T FUNCTION RIGHT BECAUSE OF THE HUMIDITY.

SO I LEFT, TURNED MY CAR RIGHT AROUND, WENT TO THAT LITTLE COFFEE CART ON BISCAYNE. I TOOK A CAFE CUBANO.

CLICK

I TIPPED NICELY, DIDN'T EVEN PULL MY GUN.

IT WAS DELICIOUS. TODAY, I DRANK THREE: ONE FOR ME, ONE FOR YOU, ONE FOR LUCK. WHAT DO YOU THINK OF THAT, RAFA?

I THINK YOU *DID* MAKE A BAD DECISION, PABLO. IF MILENA KNEW YOU LEFT YOUR POST, SHE'D STUFF THOSE SWEATY CAJONES RIGHT IN YOUR MOUTH.

CAN YOU EAT IT?

BARRACUDA? NO, IT'S A TROPHY FISH.

SHOULDA SAID SOMETHIN', CAPTAIN TOM. WOULDA LOOKED REAL GOOD ON MY WALL.

SKRRT

NICE WORK, KID. YOU MADE SHORT ORDER OF THOSE KNUCKLEHEAD ORDERLIES.

DIDN'T EVEN GET YOUR HANDS DIRTY.

JUST KEEP THIS RAD RIDE MOVING ALONG AND WE'LL BE SITTING PRETTIER THAN A PEROXIDE JOB IN A TWO-PIECE.

WHY ARE WE STOPPING? ENGINE OVERHEATED OR SOMETHING?

POP THE HOOD-- I'LL TAKE A LOOK.

YA KNOW, I WAS A MECHANIC FOR YEARS IN THE LOWER EAST SIDE. BEAT SELLING SHMATAS OUT OF A PUSHCART.

WHERE'S MY MONEY?

WHATSA MATTER? YOU DON'T TRUST ME? I'M AN HONEST BUSINESSMAN.

NO MONEY, I'M *TURNING* THIS CAR AROUND!

SURELY YOU'RE NOT SO THICK THAT YOU DON'T REALIZE YOU'RE ALREADY ANKLE DEEP IN THIS CAPER.

SUIT YOURSELF.

WOOP WOOP

COUNT IT QUICK.

NEWSPAPER...?

WHAT THE *HELL* IS THIS?!

THAT IS A LESSON--ON THE HOUSE, KID. ALWAYS COUNT THE MONEY.

YOU DON'T KNOW ME FROM ADAM. THAT'S THE OLDEST SCAM IN THE BOOK.

YOU'RE A GODDAMN CROOK!

I TOLD YOU, I'M A BUSINESSMAN.

GET ME TO CALDER RACE COURSE--YOU'LL GET YOURS.

THOUGH IN MY *HUMBLE* OPINION YOU JUST DID.

HOW DO I KNOW YOU'RE NOT LYING AGAIN?

YOU DON'T. ROLL THE DICE-- I'M THE BEST CHANCE YOU GOT.

"TRACK LOOKS KINDA SLOPPY TODAY. ONE OF THESE HORSES IS GONNA END UP AT THE GLUE FACTORY."

MILENA-- I MADE A FEW CALL--*OH!*

SORRY, LEGS, JUST YOUR OLD PAL, MEYER! ...GOOD TO HEAR YOUR PHONE IS WORKING, THOUGH!

FALL OFF A HORSE?

MEYER, YA GOTTA GET OUT OF HERE. MILENA NIEVES IS CASING THE JOINT.

WHO?

"THE GODMOTHER." SHE RUNS THE CARTELS.

NOTHING HAPPENS IN MIAMI WITHOUT HER SAY-SO.

YOU GAVE ME YOUR WORD, THAT MEANS EVERYTHING TO ME, LEGS. ...WHERE'S MY PACKAGE?

MEYER... I GOT ALL YOUR ANSWERS.

MEYER? IS THAT A NICKNAME, MORRIS?

UH--MORRIS, THIS IS NICKY TUESDAY. HE'S THE PILOT OF *THE LAZY PELICAN.*

PLEASURE TO MAKE YOUR ACQUAINTANCE, MR. TUESDAY. BUT WHY SHOULD WE BE HAVING A CONVERSATION?

YOUR PACKAGE IS IN MY BIRD'S STORAGE. SHE WENT DOWN IN ISLAMORADA.

DAMN PELICAN FLEW RIGHT INTO THE ENGINE. LUCKY I SURVIVED.

I'M SURE YOUR FAMILY IS THRILLED.

MORRIS, YOU'RE NOT GETTING IT, THIS MAN IS GOING TO GET YOU TO THE CRASH SITE--HE KNOWS ALL THE CAPTAINS DOWN IN THE KEYS.

LEGS, I DON'T HAVE TIME FOR AN ADVENTURE.

YOU WANT THE, UH, *TREASURE* WE SPOKE ABOUT?

TREASURE?

WHAT THE F-- LISTEN MORRIS, OR MEYER, OR WHATEVER THE HELL YOUR NAME IS! SO FAR YOU'VE STRUNG ME ALONG AND I HAVEN'T SEEN ONE DIME.

OPEN UP YOUR EARHOLES. YOU WANNA SHORT SOMETHING OR DO YOU WANT THE BIG PAY DAY? YOU'RE GETTIN' IN ON THE GROUND FLOOR.

HE AIN'T LYIN'. I BEEN FLYING COCAINE FOR TEN YEARS AND I NEVER SEEN A HAUL LIKE THIS.

WHAT'S THIS ABOUT COCAINE, LEGS? YOU KNOW I DON'T GET MIXED UP IN THAT STUFF.

I GOT YOU COVERED. LISTEN TO NICKY.

A WISE MAN HEARS ONE WORD AND UNDERSTANDS TWO.

SOME KID, A HOBBLING OLD MAN, AND SOME BASURA BLANCO JUST LEFT LEGS' BOX.

OLD MAN'S HOBBLING? TREAT 'IM LIKE A LIMP HORSE.

ONCE HE STUMBLES BY, PUT ONE IN THE BACK OF HIS HEAD.

FORGIVE ME MY SINS, O'LORD--

FORGIVE ME THE SINS OF MY YOUTH AND THE SINS OF MINE AGE--

CLAP

--THE SINS OF MY SOUL AND THE SINS OF MY BODY--

TLACK

LOOK AT THAT PORSCHE 911-- WHAT A BADASS.

MORE LIKE A HORSE'S ASS.

LET'S GET TO YOUR CAR AND SKEDADDLE.

ONCE WE FIND MY PAL CAPTAIN BASS DOWN IN ISLAMORADA, HE'LL SHUTTLE US RIGHT TO THE CRASH SITE.

YOU GOT NUTHIN' TO WORRY ABOUT--YOUR PAPERS WERE PRACTICALLY ON MY LAP WH--

NEED ANY HELP WITH THOSE BAGS, NICKY?

GOT PLENTY OF ROOM IN THE TRUNK.

YEAH? GOOD. I THINK I'LL BE MORE COMFORTABLE IN STEERAGE.

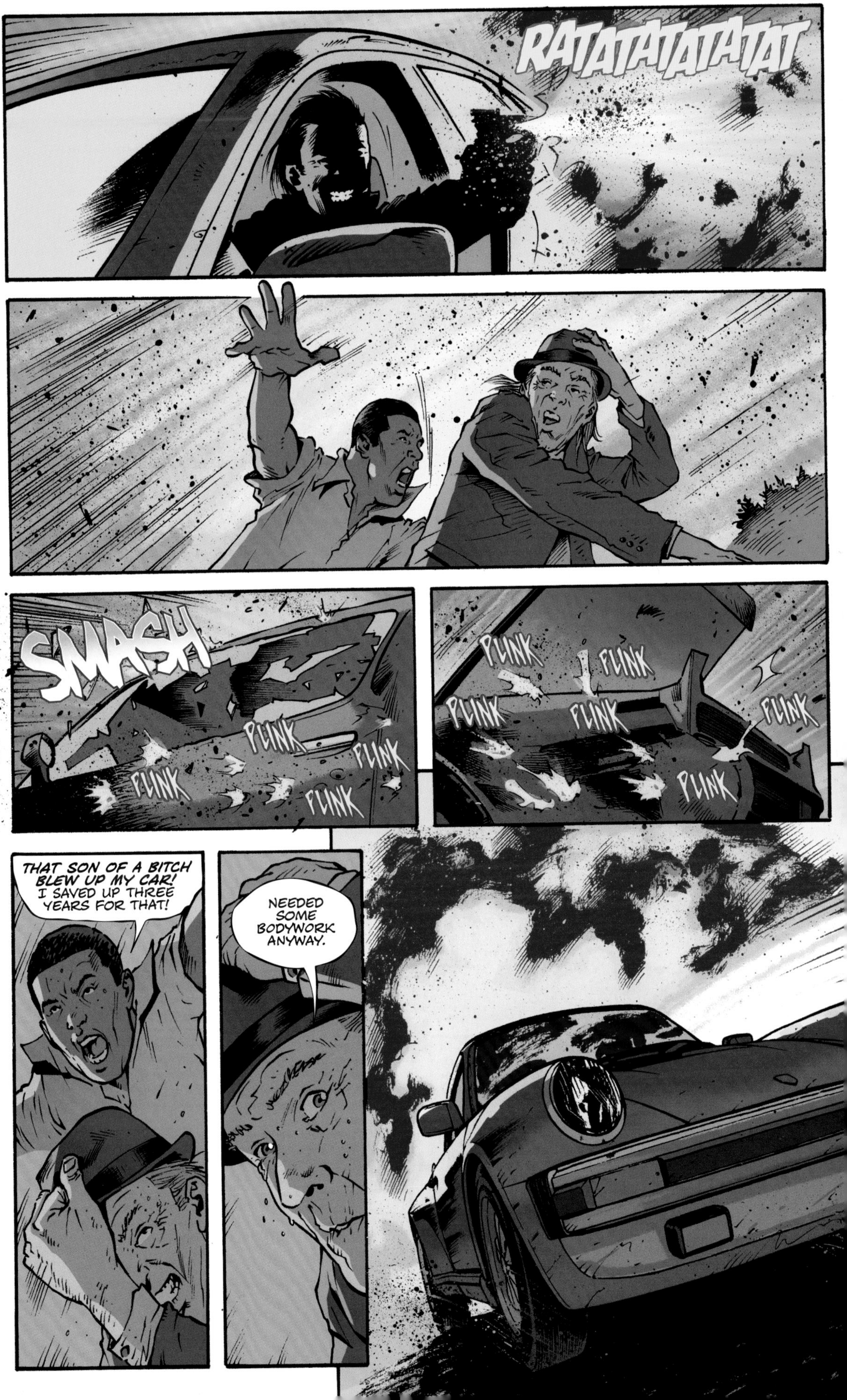
RATATATATATAT
SMASH
PLINK
FLINK
FLINK
FLINK
PLINK
FLINK
PLINK
FLINK
PLINK
PLINK
THAT SON OF A BITCH BLEW UP MY CAR! I SAVED UP THREE YEARS FOR THAT!
NEEDED SOME BODYWORK ANYWAY.

YOU JUST SURVIVED A HIT AND ARE *COMPLAINING?!*

YOU SHOULD BE SITTIN' IN A SYNAGOGUE.

BESIDES-- YOU'RE DOING A HELLUVA LOT BETTER THAN HIM.

OUR TOUR GUIDE'S CLOSED UP SHOP.

WE GOTTA ANKLE BEFORE THE COPPERS SHOW.

LISTEN TO ME--

UNLESS YOU WANT TO END UP LIKE THAT-- PIPE DOWN.

SEE THAT YELLOW CAR OVER THERE?

THE PINTO?

THOSE CARS SUCK.

YEAH, WELL THAT'S YOUR NEW HEAP.

PINTO IS LESS SUSPICIOUS THAN THIS "RAD RIDE" OF YOURS ANYWAY.

THAT CAR LOOKS LIKE A URINAL ON WHEELS.

NOT A SCRATCH--TOLD YOU I WAS A SMART BET.

HAND ME THAT TOOL BOX. I'LL BRING THE CAR AROUND.

LOOK OUT THE PASSENGER WINDOW TOO LONG--LIFE WILL ROLL RIGHT BY.

VROOM

RRRRRRRRRR

Enrique Diaz

WHOAH...
YOU OKAY?

WHAT
HAPPENED?

YA KNOW--
MIAMI
DRIVERS?

AYE, KID! YOU
OUT HERE TO CHASE
SKIRTS OR EARN
SOME SCRATCH?

HIT THE
TRUNK.

YOU DAMES
SHOULD VAMOOSE
BEFORE YOU MISS
HAPPY HOUR.

FIRST
ROUND'S
ON ME. TELL
'EM YOU'RE
A GUEST
OF LEGS
FEINSTEIN.

QUIT
CHASIN'
SKIRTS,
LET'S SEE
SOME
OF THEM
LOCK-
PICKIN'
SKILLS.

HEY,
THEY
STOPPED
ME.

MUST BE
MY SEMITIC GOOD
LOOKS.

ALL RIGHT, VALENTINO, PUT A PIN IN IT AND GET THAT LICENSE PLATE OFF YOUR CAR.

GRAB YOUR REGISTRATION-- ANYTHING WITH YOUR NAME ON IT.

I'D SAY CAR INSURANCE, BUT I KNOW CUBANS DON'T HAVE ANY IN MIAMI.

DAMN, THE ELDERLY REALLY ARE MORE RACIST.

IT'S GOTTA BE A CLEAN LIFT-- NO EVIDENCE. YOU READY?

ONE...

TWO...

THREE!

THUCK

ARE THOSE HIS *BRAINS?!*

THEY AIN'T MATZAH BALLS.

LEAVE IT. WE'LL SAY *KADDISH** ON THE ROAD. CLOSE UP THAT TRUNK.

*JEWISH MOURNER'S PRAYER

GET THE ENGINE RUNNING.

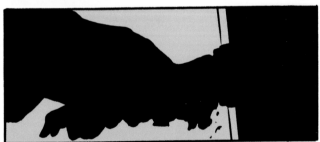

HSSSSSSS

BOOOM

HAVEN'T SEEN FIREWORKS LIKE THAT SINCE THEY LEVELED THE SANDS HOTEL.

HOW CAN YOU BE SO CALM?!

I TRUST IN THE NUMBERS. ONE AND ONE ALWAYS EQUALS TWO-- NO MATTER WHAT.

WHAT DOES THAT EVEN *MEAN*?

MATH IS ABSOLUTE *CAUSATION*-- THERE'S NO ROOM FOR DISCUSSION.

THE NUMBERS JUST ARE.

THERE'S SOMETHIN' BEAUTIFUL IN THAT.

YOU SEE THAT CROWD? COPS ARE GONNA BE SWARMING.

YOU'RE WELCOME. I JUST DELIVERED A HELLUVA DISTRACTION AND BOUGHT US SOME TIME.

"PRINTS DON'T LIFT TOO EASY AFTER A BLAZE LIKE THAT."

RRRRR

KEEP YOUR LIP BUTTONED.

IS THERE A PROBLEM, OFFICER?

WELL, I'M NOT AN OFFICER-- I'M SECURITY. BUT I DO CARRY A GUN.

IT'S MIAMI... OF COURSE YOU DO.

HOW CAN I HELP YOU?

WELL, WE'RE STOPPING ALL CARS TO SEE IF THEY SAW ANYTHING-- SUSPICIOUS.

YOU DON'T SAY.

TO BE PERFECTLY HONEST, I WAS TOO BUSY LUGGING A DEAD BODY INTO THE BACK OF MY TRUNK TO NOTICE ANYTHING.

BUT IF I HEAR ANYTHING, YOU'LL BE THE FIRST TO KNOW.

A DEAD BODY...THAT'S HILARIOUS.

WELL, BEST OF LUCK SOLVING YOUR CAPER.

IF I WERE YOU, I'D DITCH THE TRACK AND GET INTO THE ACADEMY. YOU GOT TOO MUCH SLEUTH IN YOU TO DRIVE A GOLF CART IN CIRCLES ALL DAY.

FLAASH

THIS ONE'S
FOR HIS FAMILY--
LEAVE IT IN THEIR
MAILBOX.

PABLO,
TAKE CARE OF HIS
FRIEND.

SMACK

I HAVE A WI--

BLAM

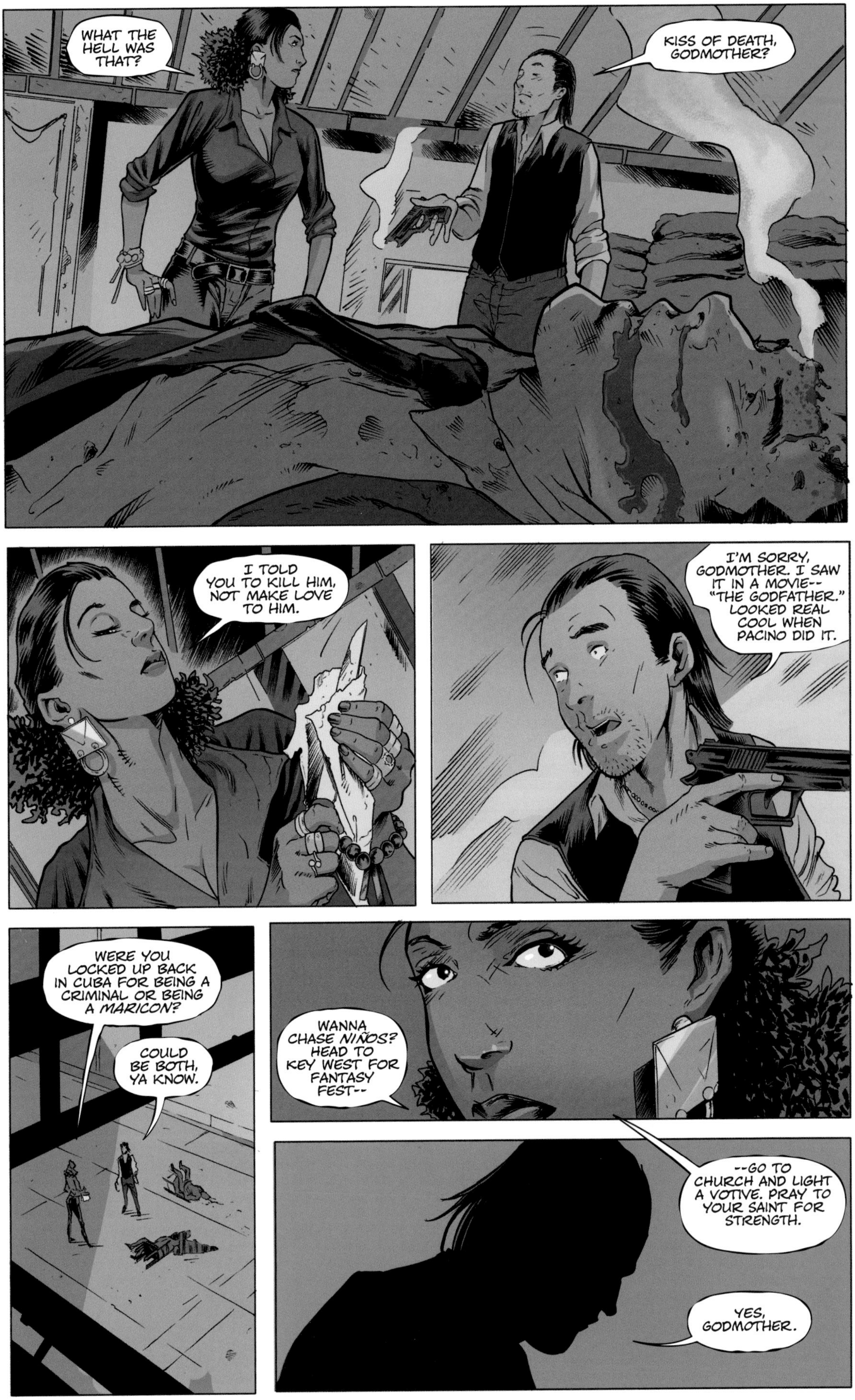
WHAT THE HELL WAS THAT?
KISS OF DEATH, GODMOTHER?
I TOLD YOU TO KILL HIM, NOT MAKE LOVE TO HIM.
I'M SORRY, GODMOTHER. I SAW IT IN A MOVIE-- "THE GODFATHER." LOOKED REAL COOL WHEN PACINO DID IT.
WERE YOU LOCKED UP BACK IN CUBA FOR BEING A CRIMINAL OR BEING A *MARICON*?
COULD BE BOTH, YA KNOW.
WANNA CHASE *NIÑOS*? HEAD TO KEY WEST FOR FANTASY FEST--
--GO TO CHURCH AND LIGHT A VOTIVE. PRAY TO YOUR SAINT FOR STRENGTH.
YES, GODMOTHER.

DRINK UP, KID. THAT'LL SETTLE YOUR STOMACH.

THIS IS DISGUSTING.

CAN'T HAVE YOU PUKING IN THE CAR. WE GOT A RIDE AHEAD.

WHAT THE HELL WAS ALL THAT ABOUT THE BODY? ARE YOU INSANE?!

WHEN YOU GOT AN ACE IN YOUR HAND MOST PEOPLE READ BLUFF.

THAT'S THE FUNNY THING ABOUT THE TRUTH--PEOPLE RARELY BELIEVE IT.

THEY'LL DOWN A LIE LIKE A SHOT OF BOURBON, BUT TRUTH--PEOPLE ARE ALLERGIC TO THE STUFF.

THERE'S YOUR LESSON FOR THE DAY.

NOW, GO SWAP OUT YOUR PLATE.

THE ENDLESS SUMMER
RAD RIDE

WHO THE *HELL* DO YOU THINK YOU ARE? I DON'T WORK FOR YOU.

YOU ALMOST GOT ME KILLED. FOR WHAT?

WHY SHOULD I TRUST YOU? I DON'T EVEN KNOW YOUR NAME.

MEYER-- MEYER LANSKY.

PLEASURE TO MAKE YOUR ACQUAINTANCE.

YOU'RE...

...YOU'RE A *REAL* CRIMINAL.

I TOLD YA, I'M A BUSINESSMAN. WE'RE PARTNERS NOW.

WIPE THE MILK OFF YOUR HOOFS BEFORE YOU GET IN THE CAR.

LOOK! IT'S DAVID GREENE!

IDIOT TOOK OUT THE LIGHTS BUT FORGOT ABOUT THE CAMERAS!

SHOULD WE CALL THE COPS? RAT HIM OUT TO HIS P.O.?

YOU AND ME--WE'RE GONNA LOSE OUR JOBS OVER THIS.

GUY WITH MY BACKGROUND-- I AIN'T GETTIN' HIRED SO QUICK.

COPS ARE TOO GOOD FOR THIS KID.

I'LL CALL MY COUSIN, ENRIQUE. HE'LL HOOK US UP WITH SOME HEAT.

WE'LL TAKE CARE OF THIS OURSELVES.

WHAP

3.

*"A liar must have
a good memory."*

– Yiddish Proverb

SMELL THAT OCEAN BREEZE... GETTIN' CLOSER TO MY BIG PAYDAY.

WHAT D'YA THINK OF THE KEYS?

ISLAMORADA
VILLAGE OF ISLANDS
WELCOMES YOU

EH, KINDA TACKY.

WHY DO YOU CARE SO MUCH ABOUT KESEV?

YOU WOULDN'T GET IT.

TRY ME.

RESPECT. THAT'S WHY. TRY HAVING A MOM FOR A JANITOR AT *YOUR* SCHOOL.

DON'T BE A YUTZ.

THINK THEY'LL RESPECT YOU 'CAUSE YOU GOT MONEY? YOU'RE A JEW, DAVID. DON'T FORGET THAT.

WHAT'S THAT HAVE TO DO WITH ANYTHING?

POMPANO
DIVE CENTER

IT'S EVERYTHING. MAKE TOO MUCH MONEY, "LOOK AT THAT KIKE-- HE MUST KNOW SOME YID BANKERS."

DON'T MAKE ENOUGH MONEY? YOU'RE JUST A RAT IN THE STREETS.

I DON'T KNOW WHERE YOU GET THIS CRAP.

KNOW YOUR HISTORY. SPAIN, ITALY, POLAND-- I HAD TO GET THE HELL OUT OF GRODNO WHEN THE NAZIS WERE AT THE GATES.

ONE THING A JEW NEEDS IS GOOD LUGGAGE 'CAUSE YOU NEVER KNOW WHEN YOU'LL HAVE TO HIGHTAIL IT OUT.

SO ENJOY THE SCENERY WHILE YOU CAN, DAVID.

A COUPLE'A IMMIGRANT JEWS LIKE US, WE'LL ALWAYS BE TOURISTS JUST PASSING THROUGH.

I DIDN'T EVEN HAVE A BAR MITZVAH.

YOU KNOW, YOU SOUND AS PARANOID AS MY MOTHER TALKING ABOUT CASTRO.

SHE ALWAYS THINKS SOMEONE'S AFTER HER.

Sapolsky's Bait&Tackle

Cold beer Sodas

SOUNDS LIKE A PRETTY SMART LADY.

FINE, WHILE YOU'RE BOTH RUNNING AWAY FROM GHOSTS--

HEY! WATCH IT!

--I'LL GET *PAID* IN THE PRESENT.

VROOM

VROOM

ASSHOLE!

THUMP

KEEP YOUR EYES ON THE ROAD.

RELAX-- I DIDN'T SEE YOU.

DIDN'T SEE ME, HUH?

VROOM VROOM

SMASH

NOW YA SEE ME?

I TOLD YOU TO LAY LOW!

WHAT, YA THINK THESE GUYS ARE ANTI-SEMITIC TOO?!

WHO KNOWS? BUT I THINK YOU'RE A TERRIBLE DRIVER.

WHAT DO I DO?

GET THAT ENGINE GOING.

ARE YOU KIDDING?

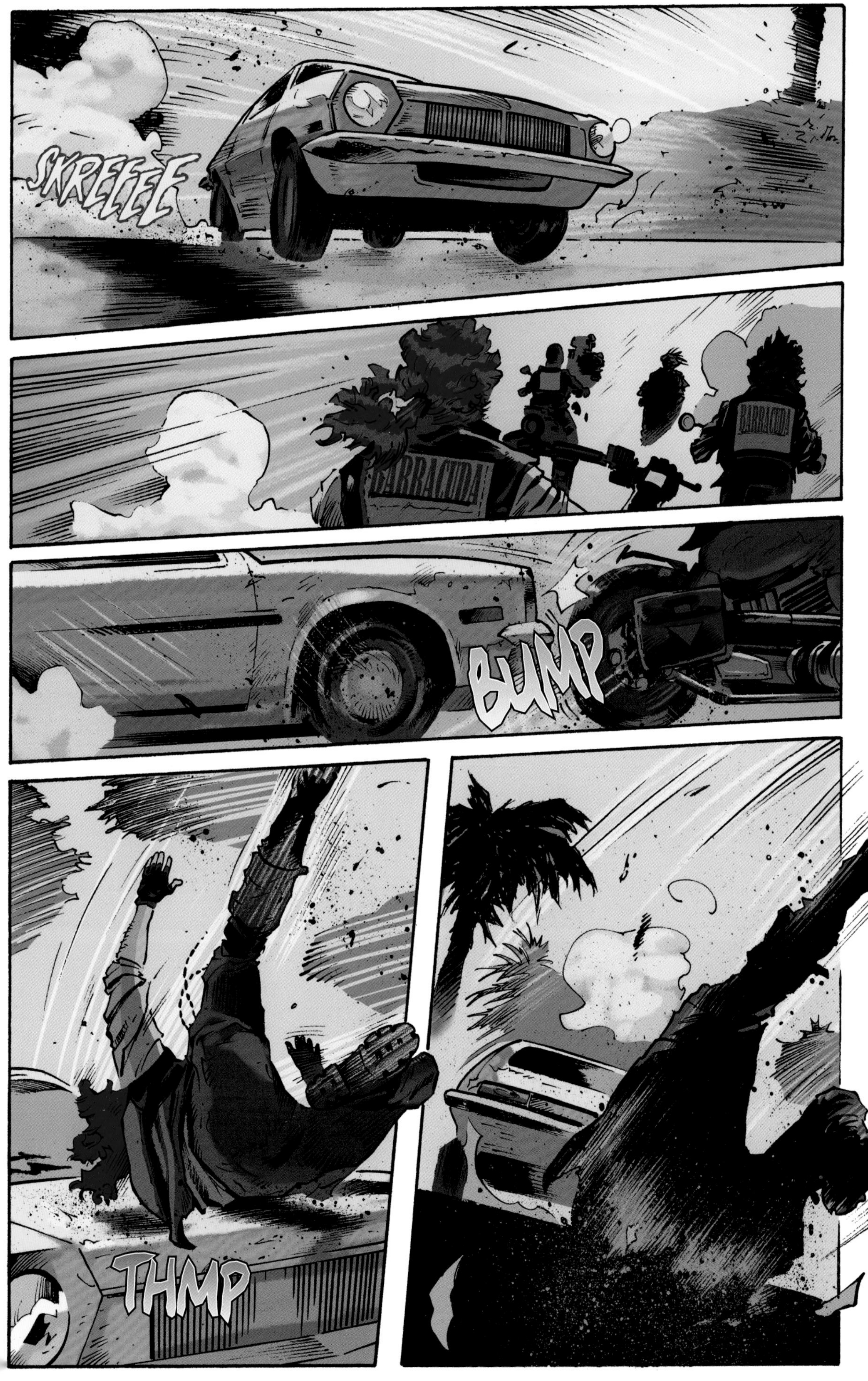
SKREEEEE
BARRACUDA
BARRACUDA
BUMP
THMP

WHATS'A MATTER WITH YOU? YOU ALMOST KILLED THAT GUY!

YOU TOLD ME TO DRIVE INTO THEM!

I MEANT PUT A SCARE INTO THEM. Y'THINK I'M SOME KINDA *ANIMAL?*

SMAASH

YOU REALLY *CAN* SMELL THE OCEAN.

GIVE ME A NAME.

≳KOFF≲

I TOLD YA EVERYTHING I KNOW--

MAYBE THIS LANGOSTA WILL GET SOME TRUTH OUTTA YOU.

TALK, TOMMY BOY, OR MY LITTLE FRIEND HERE WILL SNIP OFF YOUR PINGA.

GIVE IT A LI'L CAP'N CRUNCH!

WAIT!

EVER SINCE CAPTAIN BASS HAS BEEN HUNTING FOR MINERVA, HE HASN'T BEEN THE SAME.

WHO'S THIS LADY... MINERVA?

SHE AIN'T A LADY--SHE'S A TARPON. A FISH. SHE'S ONE OF THE OLDEST IN ISLAMORADA.

WHO GETS OBSESSED WITH A FISH?

AIN'T YOU EVER READ MOBY DICK?

FIND CAPTAIN BASS OR THE NEXT THING I READ WILL BE YOUR OBITUARY IN EL NUEVO HERALD. ¿COMPRENDE?

SHOULD I GET THE CORNED BEEF OR THE PASTRAMI? I DUNNO THE DIFFERENCE.

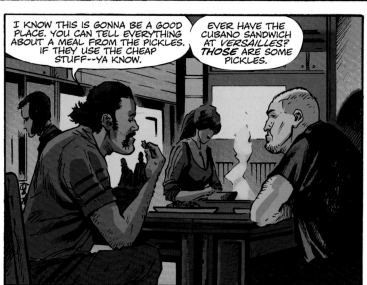

I KNOW THIS IS GONNA BE A GOOD PLACE. YOU CAN TELL EVERYTHING ABOUT A MEAL FROM THE PICKLES. IF THEY USE THE CHEAP STUFF--YA KNOW.

EVER HAVE THE CUBANO SANDWICH AT *VERSAILLES*? *THOSE* ARE SOME PICKLES.

I DON'T GIVE A *DAMN* ABOUT THE PICKLES! IF WE DON'T FIND THAT KID AND THE OLD MAN *SOMEONE'S* GONNA SQUEAL ABOUT OUR LITTLE PILL HUSTLE!

KEEP YOUR EYES ON THE DOOR FOR MY COUSIN ENRIQUE. HE'S BRINGING SOME *REAL* FIREPOWER.

OKAY...OKAY. WHICH ONE IS MORE LIKE *LENGUA*? I LOVE THE STUFF-- THE ONLY MEAT THAT TASTES YOU BACK.

JUST 'CAUSE WE'RE LOOKING FOR THAT OLD JEW DON'T MEAN YOU HAVE TO *ACT* LIKE ONE.

MAN, I'M TRYING TO GET INSIDE HIS HEAD. THAT'S WHAT IT'S ALL ABOUT. THEY SAY THE BEST COPS THINK LIKE CRIMINALS, YA KNOW.

NUTHIN' TO SAY?

YOU GOT NO SENSE OF HUMOR.

ORDER FOR ME. I'M HITTIN' THE *BAÑO*.

NOW THE ONLY THING A GAMBLER NEEDS IS A SUITCASE AND A TRUNK. AND THE ONLY TIME HE'S SATISFIED IS WHEN HE'S ON A DRUNK.

I WAS LISTENING TO THAT. DRIVER PLAYS DJ-- PRETTY STANDARD RULE.

MODERATE CHOP IN THE EVENING...SWELLS ARE SUPPOSED TO REACH FOUR TO FIVE FEET.

KID, WHEN YOU'RE A TOURIST, YOU GOTTA TRY TO SPEAK THE LANGUAGE.

WE WANT INTEL, GOTTA MAKE SOME CHIT-CHAT FIRST. FARSHTAY?

I GET YOU. TALK FISHING WITH THE FISHERMAN.

PRECISELY.

WHAT THE HELL ARE YOU DOING?

I'M "LEARNING THE LANGUAGE."

HE'S AS LOST AS YOU ARE.

KID, YOU'RE MAKING A MISTAKE. WE GOTTA DITCH THIS RIDE.

SHOWS WHAT YOU KNOW. CHECK OUT HIS SKIN--HE'S BEEN ON THE WATER.

THANK GOD. I LOST MY MATES--THEY TOOK OFF IN THE DEAD OF NIGHT. STUCK ME WITH THE HOTEL BILL. YOU HEADIN' TO KEY WEST?

WE'RE HEADING SOUTH.

THAT'LL DO JUST FINE.

A.C. BROKEN?

HIT A COUPLE OF ROUGH PATCHES OUT HERE.

♪ AND THE ONLY TIME HE'S SATISFIED IS WHEN HE'S ON A DRUNK. ♫

HEARD FROM LEGS FEINSTEIN THAT YOU BEEN ASKING ABOUT THE OLD MAN AND THE KID.

THAT'S A STUPID QUESTION.

YOU'RE OUTTA YER LEAGUE HERE.

BE A SMART GUY-- CRAWL BACK UNDER YOUR ROCK.

WHAM

THAT HARD HEAD WILL ONLY GET YOU INTO TROUBLE.

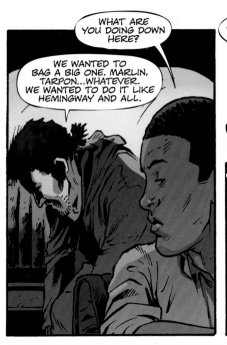

WHAT ARE YOU DOING DOWN HERE?

WE WANTED TO BAG A BIG ONE. MARLIN, TARPON...WHATEVER. WE WANTED TO DO IT LIKE HEMINGWAY AND ALL.

AND DID YOU RENT A BOAT OR CHARTER ONE?

CHARTER, OF COURSE.

LAST TIME MY ANCESTORS STEERED A SHIP THEY WERE HIGHTAILING IT AWAY FROM THE CONTINENT.

WHO WAS YOUR CAPTAIN?

OH, CAPTAIN BASS. HE'S THE BEST. HE BRINGS A LITTLE SOMETHING EXTRA TO THE PARTY.

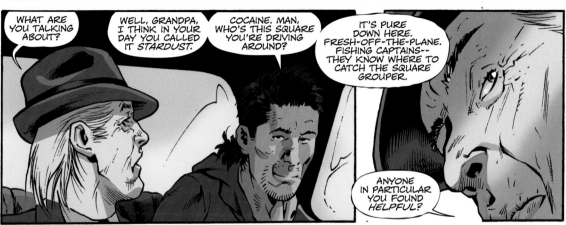

WHAT ARE YOU TALKING ABOUT?

WELL, GRANDPA, I THINK IN YOUR DAY YOU CALLED IT STARDUST.

COCAINE. MAN, WHO'S THIS SQUARE YOU'RE DRIVING AROUND?

IT'S PURE DOWN HERE. FRESH-OFF-THE-PLANE. FISHING CAPTAINS-- THEY KNOW WHERE TO CATCH THE SQUARE GROUPER.

ANYONE IN PARTICULAR YOU FOUND HELPFUL?

TURN UP THAT HEARING AID-- CAPTAIN BASS IS THE BEST. BUT IN A PINCH, SHOULD BE ABLE TO SCORE AT THE HOG'S BREATH SALOON. BIKERS ARE USUALLY CARRYING.

BUT YOU CAN NEVER TELL WHAT SOMEONE'S PACKING.

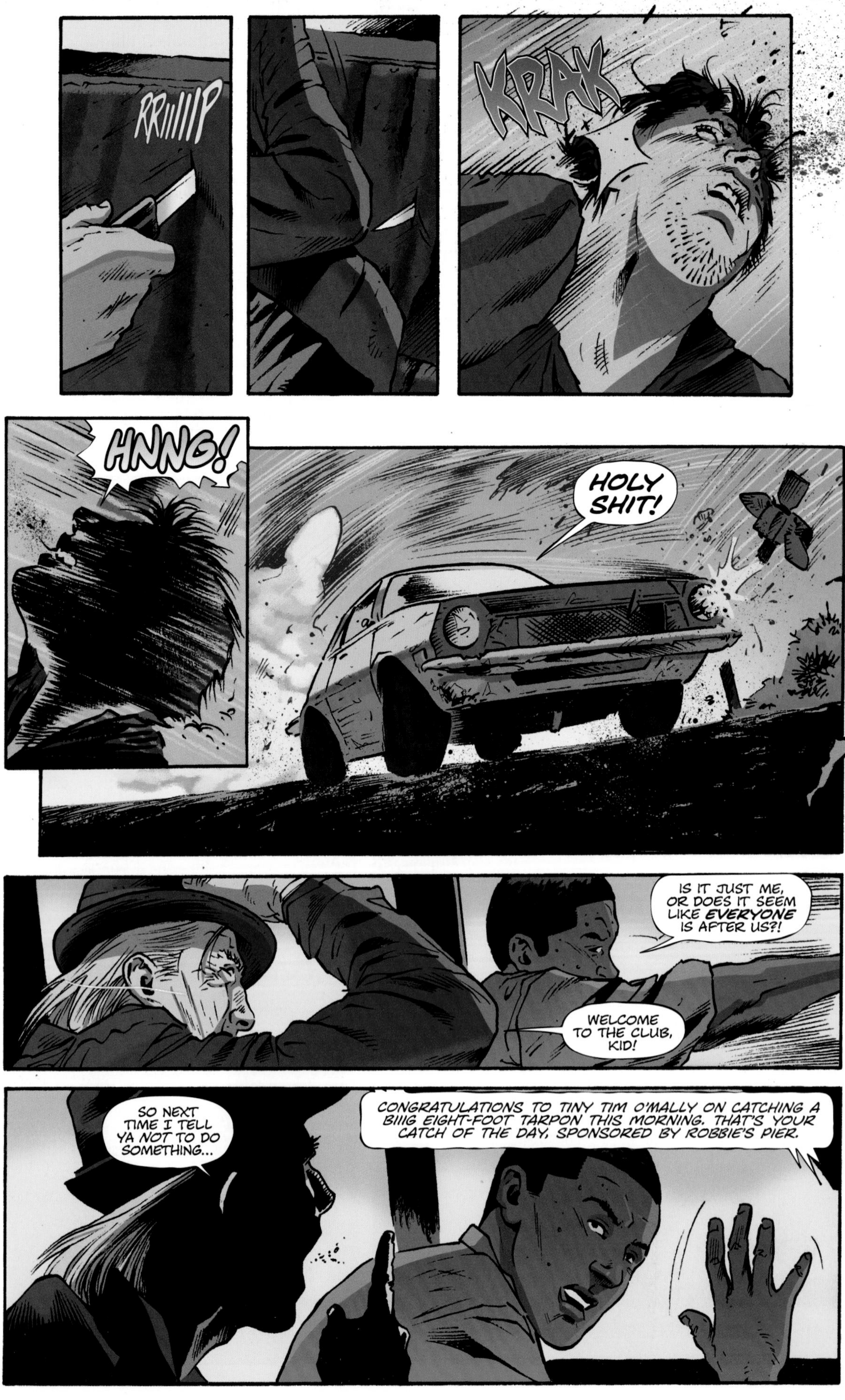
RRIIIIIP
KRAK
HNNG!
HOLY SHIT!
IS IT JUST ME, OR DOES IT SEEM LIKE EVERYONE IS AFTER US?!
WELCOME TO THE CLUB, KID!
SO NEXT TIME I TELL YA NOT TO DO SOMETHING...
CONGRATULATIONS TO TINY TIM O'MALLY ON CATCHING A BIIIG EIGHT-FOOT TARPON THIS MORNING. THAT'S YOUR CATCH OF THE DAY, SPONSORED BY ROBBIE'S PIER.

ROBBIE'S

VAMONOS, BAIT GIRL.

TARPON FEEDING

WE GAVE *THAT CABRÓN* A CHANCE TO TALK...THEN HE COULDN'T.

GO AHEAD... FEED THE FISH.

WHATCHOO GOT TO SAY FOR YOURSELF?

I TOLD YOU... *NOBODY'S* SEEN CAPTAIN BASS IN WEEKS.

YA USED SOME BAIT--GOT THAT FISH OUT OF THE WATER.

FIND CAPTAIN BASS OR YOU'RE FISH FOOD. ¿COMPRENDE?

I'LL... HE'LL BE BACK ON THE PIER.

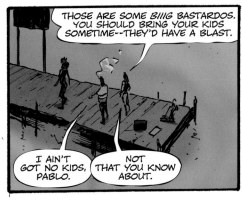

THOSE ARE SOME B/I/IG BASTARDOS. YOU SHOULD BRING YOUR KIDS SOMETIME--THEY'D HAVE A BLAST.

I AIN'T GOT NO KIDS, PABLO.

NOT THAT YOU KNOW ABOUT.

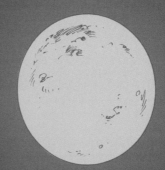

ISLAMORADA.
FLORIDA.

EVERYBODY'S GOT A PAST.

IF YOU'VE GOT A PULSE, YOU'VE HURT SOMEBODY.

SAYING I'M SORRY-- THAT'S EASY. THE WORDS DON'T MEAN A WHOLE HEAP.

L'CHAIM.

AAH!

NEVER LEAVE PRINTS, KID.

YOU WANNA FEEL BETTER? DON'T GO TO A PRIEST, A RABBI, A HEADSHRINKER.

HERE GOES NOTHING.

TO GET LASTING PEACE--
PACK YOUR VALISE AND MOVE ON.

YOU READY, KID?

I THINK THIS IS REALLY MESSED UP.

YA GOT A BETTER PLAN?

HE'S STILL ALIVE, YA KNOW.

YEAH? I'D LIKE TO STAY THAT WAY TOO. SO PUSH.

KEEP IT UNDER YOUR HAT.

SPLASH

HOPEFULLY, GET A LITTLE SECHEL-- A LITTLE WISDOM OUT OF THE DEAL.

NICE WORK, KID.

WHERE'D YOU PUT MY VALISE?

...

IT'S IN THE BACK SEAT.

SOMEONE'S GOIN' FOR A DIP IN THE DRINK!

IT'S UP TO YOU, BUT IT'S BEST TO TRAVEL LIGHT.

THIS WAS YOUR STUPID IDEA.

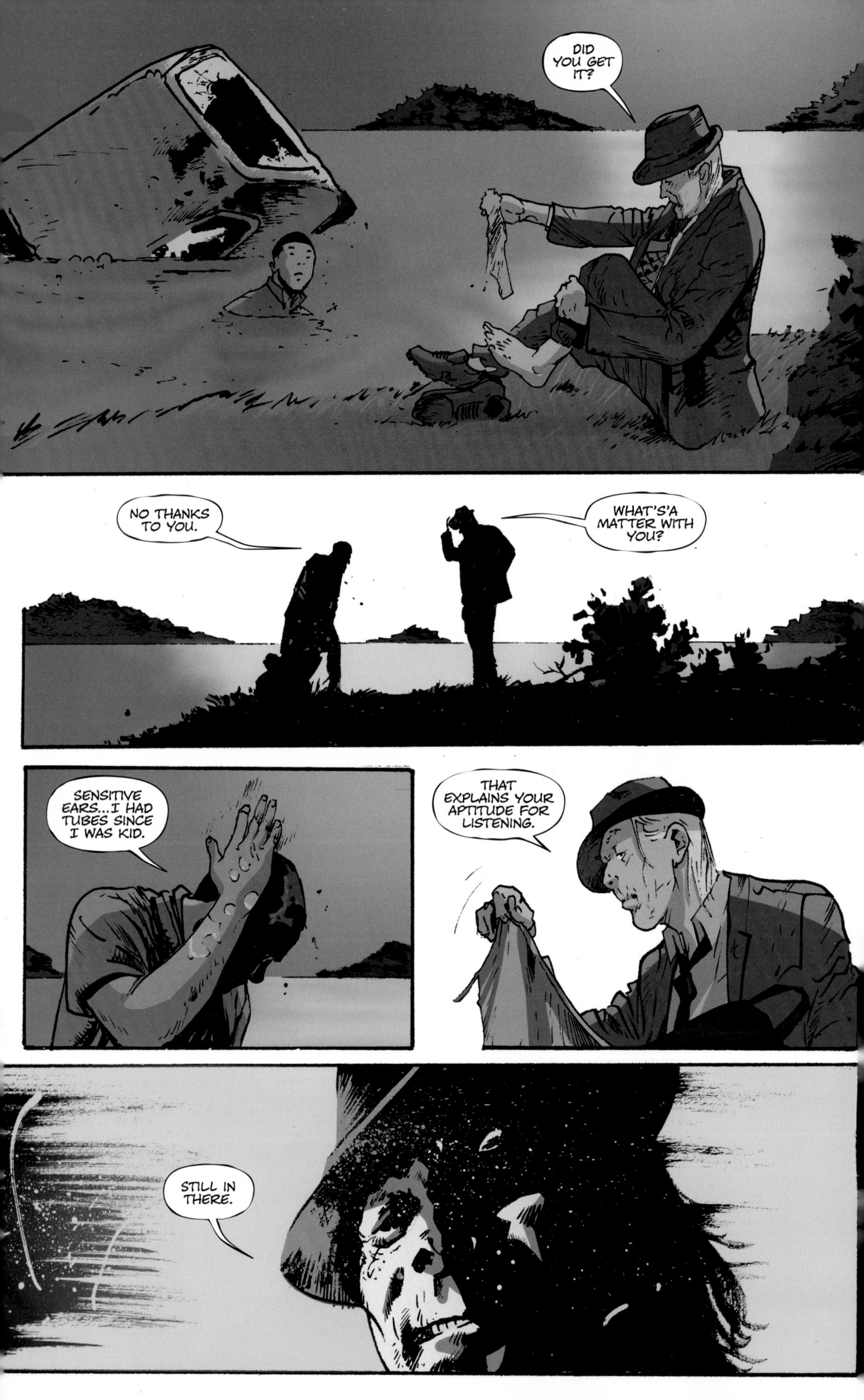
DID YOU GET IT?
NO THANKS TO YOU.
WHAT'S'A MATTER WITH YOU?
SENSITIVE EARS...I HAD TUBES SINCE I WAS KID.
THAT EXPLAINS YOUR APTITUDE FOR LISTENING.
STILL IN THERE.

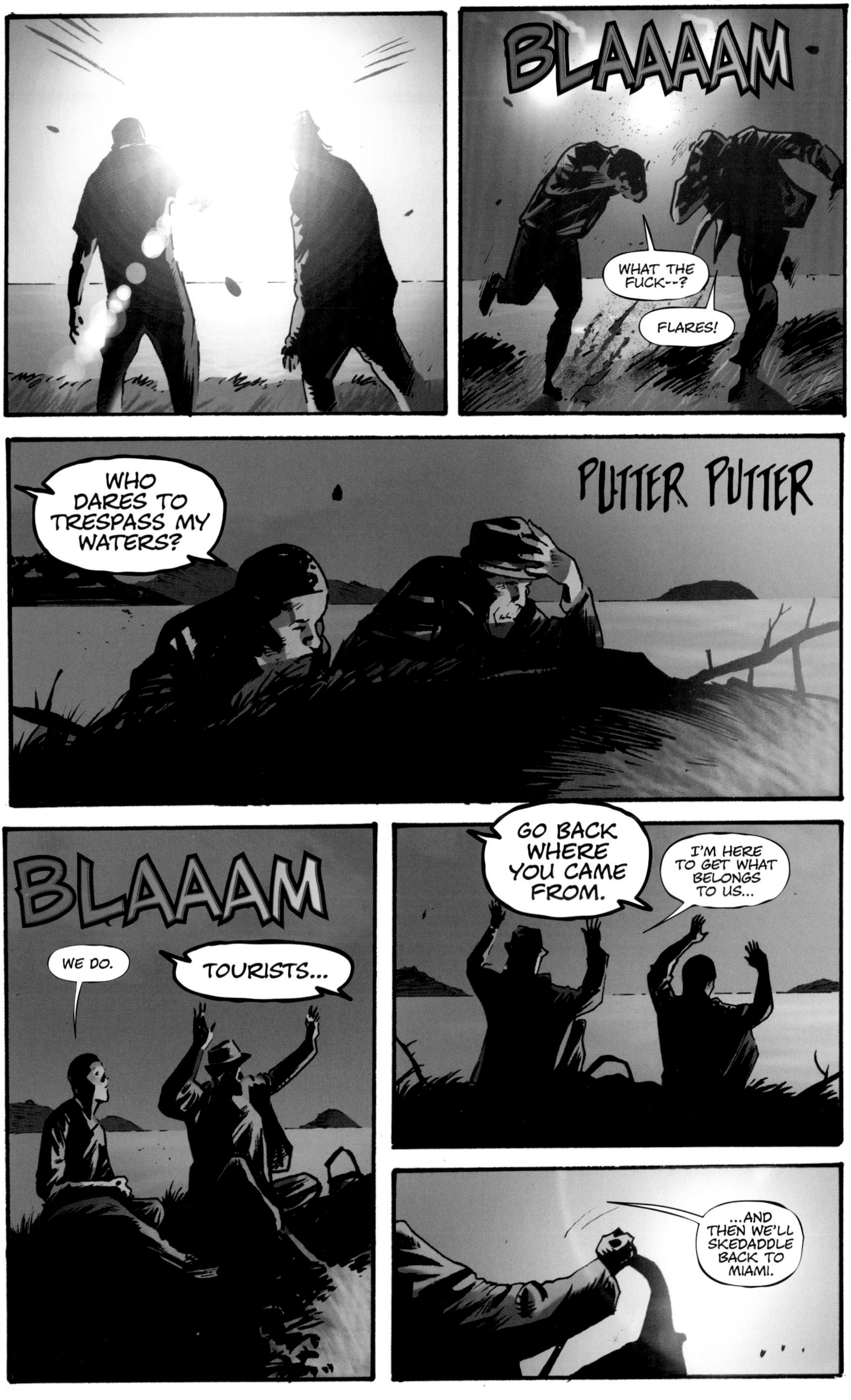
BLAAAAM
WHAT THE FUCK--?
FLARES!
PUTTER PUTTER
WHO DARES TO TRESPASS MY WATERS?
BLAAAM
TOURISTS...
WE DO.
GO BACK WHERE YOU CAME FROM.
I'M HERE TO GET WHAT BELONGS TO US...
...AND THEN WE'LL SKEDADDLE BACK TO MIAMI.

Lookout Below

WHAT THE HELL WAS THAT ABOUT?

PROOF WE'RE NOT THE ENEMY--

DON'T BE A DUMPKOFF*. WE JUST FOUND CAPTAIN BASS.

*DUNCE

4.

"The door to evil is wide, but the return gate is narrow."

– **Yiddish Proverb**

TODAY.

CAPTAIN BASS ALMOST KILLED ME, LEGS.

YOU WANNA DO ME ANY MORE *FAVORS*-- I'LL PASS.

MEYER, CAPTAIN BASS HE'S GOT--SHPILKES*. PEOPLE HAVE BEEN SNIFFING AROUND FOR HIM SINCE THE LAZY PELICAN WENT DOWN.

*A BAD CASE OF THE NERVES

THIS BETTER NOT BE A *SET-UP*, LEGS. I'LL HAUNT YOU FROM THE GRAVE.

DON'T GET SORE, MEYER. NO ONE KNOWS THAT YOU'RE DOWN THERE--OTHER THAN CAPTAIN BASS.

THEY THINK YOU'RE DEAD.

I PAID THE POLICE OFF. THEY WROTE UP A REPORT.

WHICH REMINDS ME--WHO THE HELL TOLD YOU TO BLOW UP A CAR IN MY PARKING LOT. DO YOU *KNOW* WHAT THAT'LL DO TO *MY PREMIUMS?!*

NEXT TIME YOU TELL ME THE COAST IS CLEAR--IT *BETTER* BE.

SO WHERE, PRAY TELL, IS THE RENDEZVOUS SPOT?

IT'S PERFECT, MEYER NO ONE WILL EXPECT YOU. THEATER OF THE SEA.

"THEATER OF THE SEA"? SOUNDS LIKE *BROAD DAYLIGHT*. IT'S GOT THE WORD "THEATER" RIGHT IN IT!

I *LOVE* THAT PLACE!

THEY HAVE THESE REALLY COOL, GIANT SEA TURTLES.

AT LEAST THE KID'S HAPPY.

SSHKLAK

LEGS, I DON'T THINK YOU REMEMBER THE WAY I OPERATE. YOU KEEP IT UNDER YOUR HAT-- FARSHTAY.

PLAIN SIGHT, MEYER--THAT'S THE WAY WE DO IT DOWN IN MIAMI. THERE'S SO MUCH FLASH-- NOBODY'S THE WISER.

CAPTAIN BASS GOT THE GOLDEN LURE, RIGHT? YOU'RE GOOD. HE'LL BE DROPPING ANCHOR AROUND SUNSET WITH THE OTHER BOOZE CRUISES.

BANG

LEGS, WHAT THE HELL WAS THAT?

JUST TAKING CARE OF AN OLD FRIEND.

MEYER, DON'T WORRY ABOUT YOUR PAPERS. EVERYTHING IS AIRTIGHT.

YEAH-- COFFINS ARE AIRTIGHT TOO.

CLICK

AND STAY OUT!

THUCK

THUMP

GIVE ME YOUR KEYS.

FRONT POCKET ON THE LEFT.

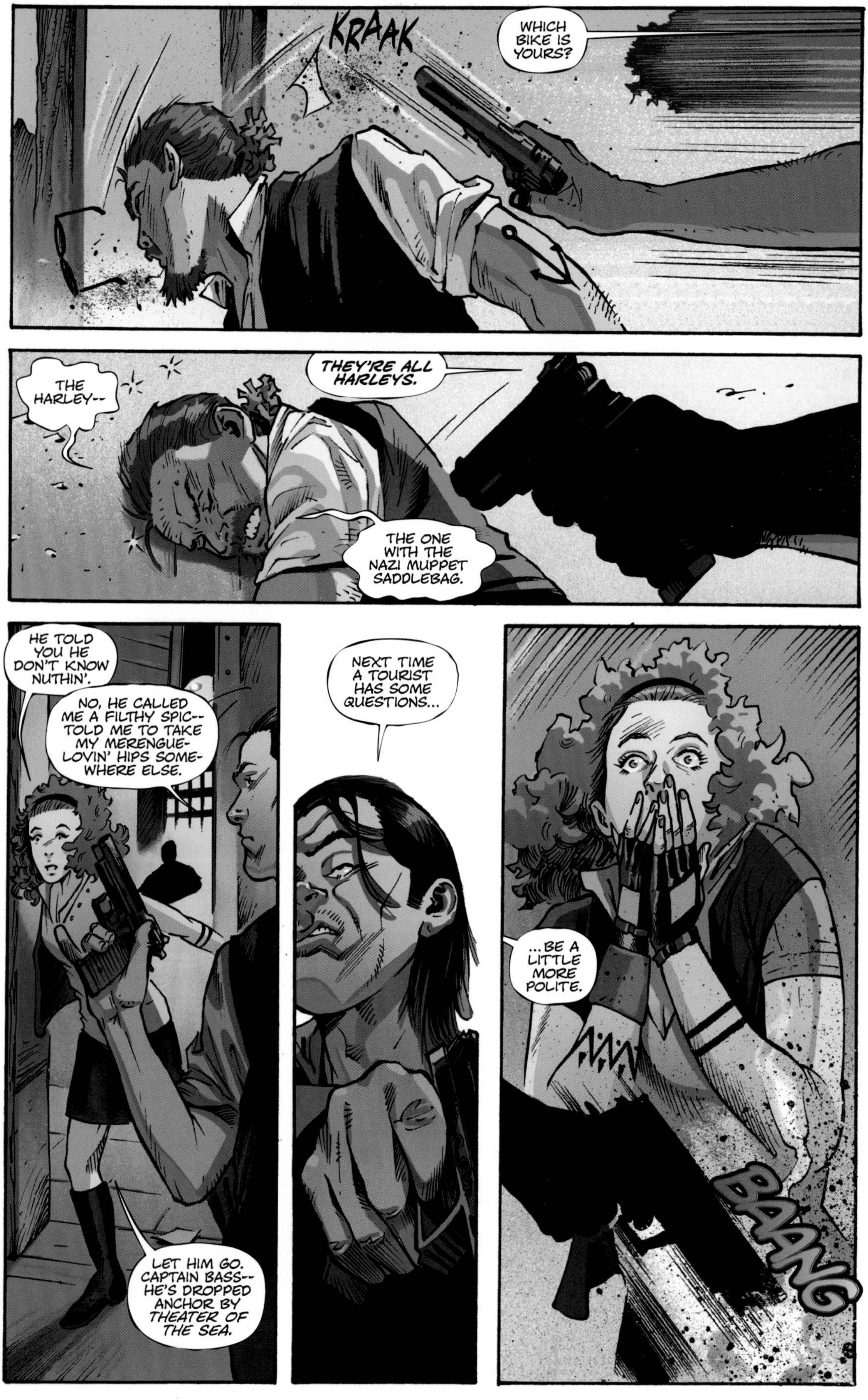
KRAAK
WHICH BIKE IS YOURS?
THE HARLEY--
THEY'RE ALL HARLEYS.
THE ONE WITH THE NAZI MUPPET SADDLEBAG.
HE TOLD YOU HE DON'T KNOW NUTHIN'.
NO, HE CALLED ME A FILTHY SPIC--TOLD ME TO TAKE MY MERENGUE-LOVIN' HIPS SOMEWHERE ELSE.
LET HIM GO. CAPTAIN BASS--HE'S DROPPED ANCHOR BY THEATER OF THE SEA.
NEXT TIME A TOURIST HAS SOME QUESTIONS...
...BE A LITTLE MORE POLITE.
BAANG

AND HOW MANY NIGHTS WILL YOU BE STAYING--

--MR. TUESDAY?

JUST THE ONE. AND IF ANYONE CALLS ASKING AROUND FOR *MORRIS GLUCK*...

...HE AIN'T HERE.

BUY THE LITTLE LADY SOMETHING NICE. NOT *TOO* NICE. PEOPLE START EXPECTING THINGS.

HEY, BENNY! BRING MY BAG TO THE ROOM.

DO I LOOK LIKE A *BELLHOP* TO YOU?

DO I GOTTA ANSWER THAT?

:SHHHHSASSH:

AFTER SPAWNING, ALL PACIFIC SALMON AND MOST ATLANTIC SALMON DIE, AND THE SALMON LIFE CYCLE STARTS OVER AGAIN.

JEEZ, NATURE IS DEPRESSING.

SURE PICKED A DUMP FOR SOMEONE WITH CASH. CHEECA LODGE IS RIGHT UP THE WAY.

SPEAKING OF CASH-- LET'S TALK HARD NUMBERS ABOUT MY PAYOUT--*HEY!* WHERE YOU GOING?

GOING TO SEE LOUIS PRIMA AT THE SAHARA. WHAT DOES IT LOOK LIKE?!

GOING TO TAKE A SCHVITZ*. I NEED TO CLEAR MY HEAD.

*SWEAT, GO TO A STEAM ROOM

ARE ALL GANGSTERS SUCH HUGE ASSHOLES?

I TOLD YOU--I'M NOT A *GANGSTER.* I'M A *BUSINESSMAN.*

ME AND THE BOYS USED TO CONTROL THE DOCKS. THOSE WORKERS LISTENED TO *US* BEFORE THE GUY SIGNING THEIR CHECKS.

NOTHING GOT IN OR OUT WITHOUT OUR SAY-SO.

THEY WANTED TO STRIKE--THEY'D GET A SHOVEL UPSIDE THE HEAD.

THIS WAS RIGHT AROUND PEARL HARBOR AFTER *THE NORMANDY* CAUGHT FIRE IN MANHATTAN AT PIER 88. THE KRAUTS COULDA DONE ANYTHING AT THE TIME.

THOSE U-BOATS--COULDN'T OPEN A COPY OF *THE NEW YORK HERALD TRIBUNE* WITHOUT SOME KINDA SUBMARINE SCARE.

SO THE U.S. NAVY ITSELF-- THEIR TOP PEOPLE-- THEY CAME TO *ME*.

THEY HELD THEIR FIVE STAR HATS IN THEIR HANDS. THEY SAID--

--"MEYER, WE NEED YOUR PEOPLE TO WATCH THE DOCKS. WE NEED YOUR WORKERS TO PROTECT NEW YORK'S HARBOR."

AND WHAT DID I SAY? I'M A PATRIOT YA KNOW--BORN ON THE 4TH OF JULY. DON'T BELIEVE IT-- CHECK MY BIRTH CERTIFICATE.

I SAID I'D DO IT. AND THEY OWED ME SOMETHING. THEY OWED ME SOMETHING *BIG*. THEY HAD TO *GUARANTEE* MY LAW OF RETURN.

GOLDA MEIR WASN'T GONNA KEEP ME OUTTA ISRAEL. VISITING MY ZEIDA AT MOUNT OF OLIVES JEWISH CEMETERY--GOING *HOME*...

...THAT'S MY *RIGHT* AS A JEW.

KSSSS

OH!

WHAT THE--?!

I KNEW YOU WERE A THIEF. HAD NO IDEA YOU WERE A SNOOP.

NOT TOO SMART TO GO DIGGING FOR DIRT ON ME.

I--I WAS JUST...

WHAAP

YOU LIED-- YOU ARE A GODDAMN CRIMINAL.

ZEY SHTIL, YOU PISSANT. I'VE DONE A LOT OF GOOD FOR A LOT OF PEOPLE.

I PROTECTED THIS COUNTRY--PUT MY NECK ON THE LINE. WHO THE HELL HAVE YOU EVER TRIED TO HELP--OTHER THAN YOURSELF?

I'M SORRY, MEYER--ALL RIGHT. I SHOULDN'T HAVE GONE THROUGH YOUR STUFF.

BUT IF YOU'RE GONNA KICK MY ASS CAN YOU AT LEAST PUT ON SOME PANTS FIRST?

HAAA CHOOO

Lime Green Key Lime Pie

THEATER OF THE SEA

BLESS YOU, ENRIQUE. THAT'S LIKE THE 10TH TIME YOU SNEEZED. ALLERGIES DON'T GET YOU NO HANDICAPPED PASS.

STOP BLESSING ME, DAMN IT. I *BOUGHT* THIS-- A SOUVENIR FROM MY PINTO.

I'M ALLERGIC TO LIGHT--ALL RIGHT. IT'S CALLED A *PHOTIC SNEEZE REFLEX.*

THAT'S WEIRD AS SHIT.

AIN'T *THAT* WEIRD. IT'S A GENETIC DISORDER 18-35 PERCENT OF MOTHERFUCKERS GOT IT.

I NEVER HEARD OF THAT...AND I WORKED IN A HOSPITAL.

DOING WHAT--CHANGING BEDPANS? YOU AIN'T NO DOCTOR HELL, YOU BARELY EVEN A NURSE.

CALLE TÉ I KNOW THE BASICS. I COULD DO CPR.

YEAH? YOU DIDN'T GIVE A DAMN ABOUT *ANYONE* IN THAT HOME.

MY COUSIN TOLD ME ABOUT THE LITTLE PILL SIDE RACKET THE TWO OF YOU WERE RUNNING--BEFORE YOU GOT HIM *KILLED.*

DON'T PIN NUTHIN' ON ME. I'M LUCKY TO BE SITTING HERE AT ALL.

ALL RIGHT THEN-- WHOSE FAULT IS IT?

THE GODMOTHER, MAN. DON'T MAKE ME SAY HER NAME.

WHEN I CAME OUTTA THE BATHROOM, HIS GODDAMN HEAD WAS MISSING! ONLY THINGS ON THE TABLE WERE A BLOODY PICKLE AND THE CHECK.

HAAA CHOOO

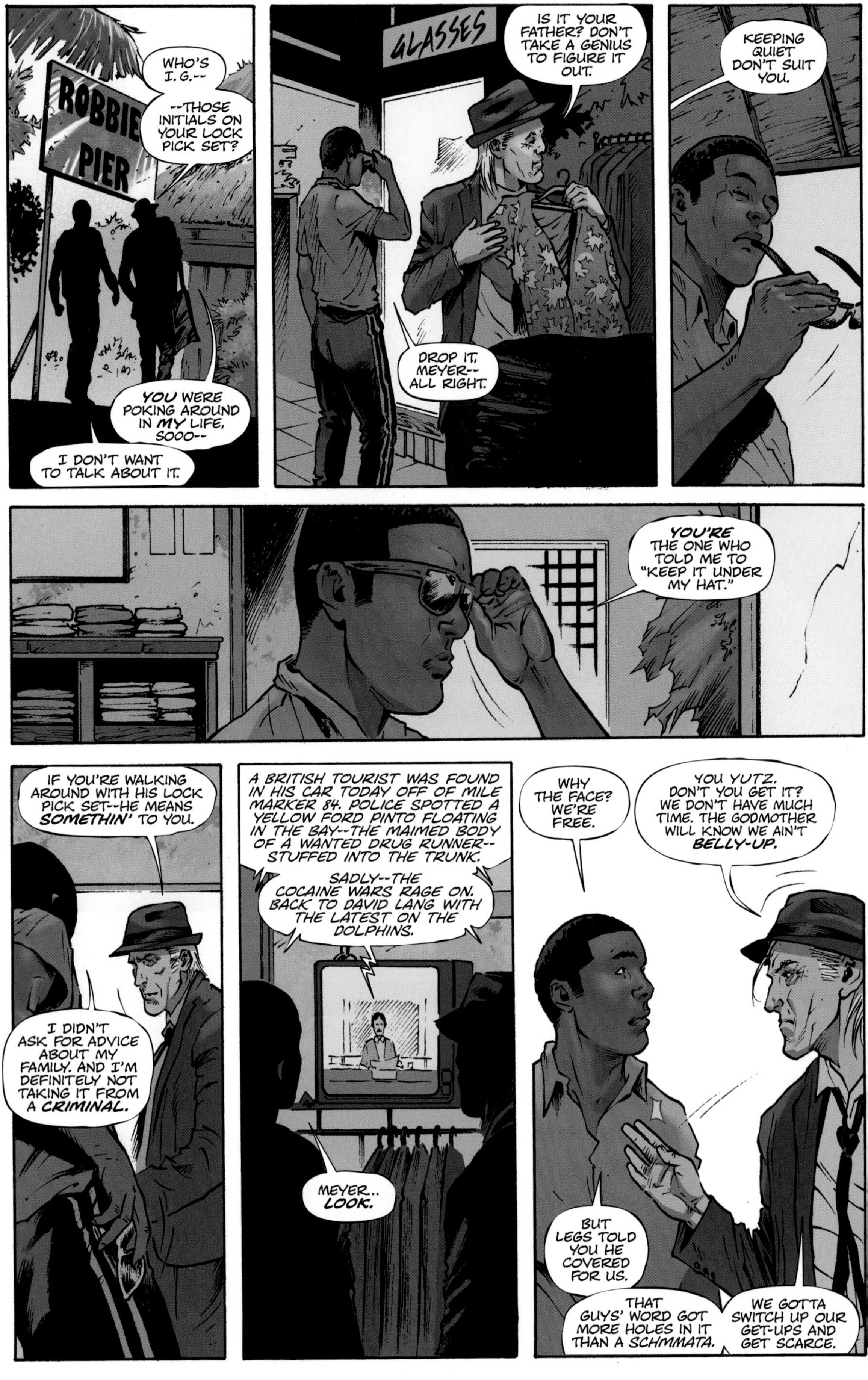
ROBBIE PIER
WHO'S I. G.--
--THOSE INITIALS ON YOUR LOCK PICK SET?
YOU WERE POKING AROUND IN MY LIFE, SOOO--
I DON'T WANT TO TALK ABOUT IT.
GLASSES
IS IT YOUR FATHER? DON'T TAKE A GENIUS TO FIGURE IT OUT.
DROP IT, MEYER-- ALL RIGHT.
KEEPING QUIET DON'T SUIT YOU.
YOU'RE THE ONE WHO TOLD ME TO "KEEP IT UNDER MY HAT."
IF YOU'RE WALKING AROUND WITH HIS LOCK PICK SET--HE MEANS SOMETHIN' TO YOU.
I DIDN'T ASK FOR ADVICE ABOUT MY FAMILY. AND I'M DEFINITELY NOT TAKING IT FROM A CRIMINAL.
A BRITISH TOURIST WAS FOUND IN HIS CAR TODAY OFF OF MILE MARKER 84. POLICE SPOTTED A YELLOW FORD PINTO FLOATING IN THE BAY--THE MAIMED BODY OF A WANTED DRUG RUNNER--STUFFED INTO THE TRUNK.
SADLY--THE COCAINE WARS RAGE ON. BACK TO DAVID LANG WITH THE LATEST ON THE DOLPHINS.
MEYER... LOOK.
WHY THE FACE? WE'RE FREE.
YOU YUTZ. DON'T YOU GET IT? WE DON'T HAVE MUCH TIME. THE GODMOTHER WILL KNOW WE AIN'T BELLY-UP.
BUT LEGS TOLD YOU HE COVERED FOR US.
THAT GUYS' WORD GOT MORE HOLES IN IT THAN A SCHMMATA.
WE GOTTA SWITCH UP OUR GET-UPS AND GET SCARCE.

BUT WE'RE GONNA PAY FOR IT, FARSHTEYN?

GO GET SOME INTEL FROM THE CHECKOUT GAL. PRICE CHECK--**GOT IT?**

YOU LOOK A LITTLE LIKE BUGSY*. DON'T LET THAT GET TO YOUR *KEPPE.* USE SOME OF THAT CHARM OF YOURS.

*BUGSY SIEGEL

HOW MUCH FOR THE SUNGLASSES?

SO STRANGE. I JUST MARKED THEM.

YOU GOT ME. WHAT I **REALLY** WANT TO KNOW ABOUT--IS **YOU.**

LISTEN, **CREEP,** IF I HAD A NICKEL FOR EVERY DRUNKEN FISHERMAN WHO THOUGHT HE HAD A SHOT AT THE BAIT GIRL--I'D HAVE ENOUGH TO BUY A PLANE TICKET TO LOS ANGELES.

YOU AN ACTRESS? YOU DO HAVE THAT...SPECIAL SOMETHING.

SURE DO LAY IT ON THICK. WHAT DO YOU WANT, CHUMP?

FINE--ME AND MY GRANDPA BACK THERE, WE'RE LOOKING TO CHARTER A BOAT. POOR GUY--CANCER. THIS MAY BE OUR LAST WEEK TOGETHER.

I WANT IT TO BE MEMORABLE SO I WANT THE BEST. I HEAR CAPTAIN BASS...

LET ME GUESS...YOU'RE FROM MIAMI, RIGHT? COUPLE OF FRIENDS OF YOURS HAVE BEEN ASKING ABOUT HIM AND THEY WERE A **HELLUVA** LOT MORE CONVINCING THAN **YOU.**

BUT--YOU **ARE** KINDA CUTE WHEN YOU'RE LYING. LAST I HEARD, HE'S BEEN DOCKING AT *THEATER OF THE SEA.*

CAREFUL. THOSE FRIENDS OF YOURS--I'VE NEVER SEEN BAD LIKE THAT.

HOW MUCH FOR TICKETS TO THE SEA LION SHOW?

INCLUDED WITH THE PRICE OF ADMISSION.

LET'S ANKLE.

LIVE A LITTLE. WE GOT AN HOUR CAPTAIN BASS ISN'T DROPPING ANCHOR UNTIL SUNSET.

IS THAT THE YID?

SURE AS HELL. WE GOTTA AIM RIGHT...PARK'S PACKED.

WHO GIVES A DAMN? THEY TOOK MY PINTO.

THUM

GIVE ME A QUARTER. I WANNA BUY SOME TURTLE FOOD.

JEEZ, KID. THIS AIN'T A CLASS FIELD TRIP.

I'M SORRY, MILITARY IDS DON'T ALLOW FREE ADMISSION TO THE PARK-- ALTHOUGH YOU DO SAVE 25%.

OKAY--I'LL TAKE THAT AAA DISCOUNT. LEMME GET MY WALLET.

BLAM

WHAT WAS THAT?

IT'S EXACTLY WHAT YOU THINK IT IS.

DAVID-- RUN!

BLAST THAT YID!

DAMMIT--

CLICK CLICK CLICK

--WATER LOGGED.

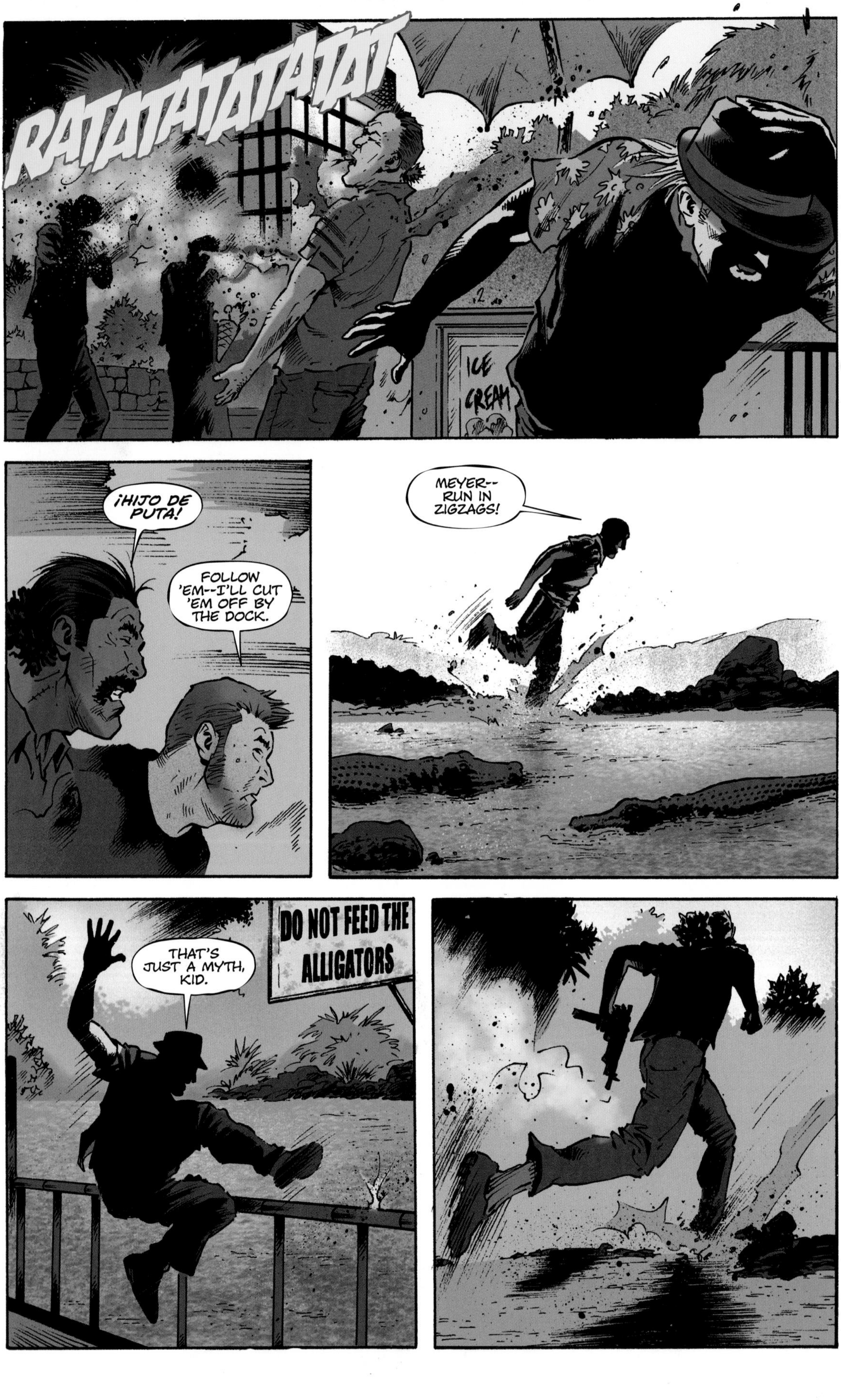
RATATATATATAT
ICE CREAM
¡HIJO DE PUTA!
FOLLOW 'EM--I'LL CUT 'EM OFF BY THE DOCK.
MEYER-- RUN IN ZIGZAGS!
DO NOT FEED THE ALLIGATORS
THAT'S JUST A MYTH, KID.

ESCUCHE. SHOW'S OVER.

RATATATATATAT

Dolphin Show

NO, PABLO. IT'S JUST STARTING.

WHOLE PLACE SMELLS LIKE GODDAMN FISH.

STINKS LESS THAN ALL THAT PACO RABANNE YOU WEAR.

HE'S PACKING.

BLAST 'EM!

RATATATATATAT

RATATATA

BRATATATAT

THOUGHT YOU TOOK CARE OF THIS BACK AT WOLFIE'S.

I TOOK CARE OF HIS EYEBROW.

THIS THE GUY?

CAN'T TELL-- AIN'T NO FOREHEAD LEFT.

WHO TOLD YOU TO JUMP INTO A GATOR PIT?!

WE'RE SCREWED.

I JUST REACTED.

NEXT TIME-- REACT *BETTER.*

HE AIN'T MUCH DIFFERENT THAN ANY OTHER BRUNO.

WANNA LITTLE BREATHING ROOM?

GIVE 'EM A ZETZ ON THE SNOUT.

BRATAT

MORRIS-- PROMISE I WON'T PUT A BULLET IN YOUR HEAD.

MY CONTRACT DON'T ALLOW ELDERLY ABUSE.

A SMART MAN KNOWS WHEN TO LEAVE MONEY ON THE TABLE. YOUR ODDS START OUT 50/50.

THEY DON'T ALWAYS STAY THAT WAY.

Theater The Sea
Marine Mammal Park
Islamorada, Florida

IN 1959, CASTRO AND HIS GOONS STARTED TAKING SLEDGEHAMMERS TO SLOT MACHINES.

RATATATATATAT

SAID THEY WERE TRYING TO DESTROY A SYMBOL OF YANKEE IMPERIALISM.

THE ODDS SHIFTED.

I LEFT 17 MILLION ON THE TABLE.

DIDN'T WANNA GET IN THE POOL?

NOW YA DO THE DEAD MAN FLOAT.

WE GOTTA HIT THE WATER!

KID, I TOLD YOU-- I DON'T SWIM!

THE SMART BET WAS TO VAMOOSE.

NOW YOU DO!

I TOOK THE LAST PLANE OUT OF HAVANA.

IF YOU REALLY WANNA COME OUT AHEAD AT THE CASINO--

RATATATATATAT

SPLASSH

EASE UP, KID.

YOU TRYING TO SAVE ME OR STRANGLE ME.

CAN'T I DO BOTH?

--THERE'S ONLY ONE WAY TO WIN.

DON'T PLAY.

PLEASE--I HELP THE ELDERLY. I *TAKE CARE* OF PEOPLE.

NOW I TAKE CARE OF YOU.

BANG

GODMOTHER, THAT WAS FANTASTIC! SO DRAMATIC.

YOU BEEN WATCHING THAT COPY OF *THE GODFATHER* I BORROWED TO YOU?

ALL THAT TV IN YOUR HEAD, PABLO--IT'S WORSE FOR YOU THAN COCAINE.

STOP SQUIRMING AROUND.

THINK I FELT A SHARK.

CAPTAIN BASS-- YOU MIGHT BE THE ONLY GUY TOUGHER TO FIND THAN ME.

PERMISSION TO BOARD, CAPTAIN?

WHATSA MATTER-- FEELING A LITTLE SEASICK THERE, CAPTAIN?

PERMISSION-- GRANTED.

5.

*"Everything ends
in weeping."*

– Yiddish Proverb

LOOKS LIKE WE CAUGHT SOME BOTTOM FEEDERS.

A COUPLE'A *JEW* FISH.

THAT A REAL FISH, PABLO?

GODDAMN RIGHT IT IS, RAFA.

OLD MAN, REMEMBER THAT SCENE IN *THE GODFATHER* WHEN THEY'RE SITTING IN THE OFFICE WITH MICHAEL CORLEONE...

I ONLY SAW THE SEQUEL WITH HYMAN ROTH.* I WASN'T TOO IMPRESSED.

*"HYMAN ROTH" IN *THE GODFATHER II* IS BASED ON MEYER LANSKY.

THEY BRING IN A PACKAGE WRAPPED IN BROWN PAPER TO SONNY.

EVERYONE LOOKS REAL CONFUSED.

THERE'S A SPEAR GUN IN STORAGE BENEATH THE LIFE VESTS.

¡CALLATÉ!

TELL 'EM WHAT HAPPENS, PABLO.

HE OPENS UP THE PACKAGE. THERE ARE TWO DEAD FISH INSIDE. TESSIO SAYS, "IT'S A MESSAGE..."

"...IT MEANS LUCA BRASI SLEEPS WITH THE FISHES."

YOUR COCAINE'S ON THIS SHIP.

CAPTAIN BASS TRIED TO MAKE OFF WITH IT.

HE'S LYING...I BEEN DOING PICK-UPS FOR YEARS! WHY WOULD I PINCH ANY OF YOUR SQUARE GROUPER *NOW?!*

HE'S JUST TRYING TO PROTECT THE KID!

TALK OR YOU'RE JOINING LUCA BRASI.

BLAM

YOU PULL THAT TRIGGER BEFORE THE KID *TALKS*, I'M GONNA LEAVE YOU FLOATIN' OUT HERE.

ENOUGH! OLD SCHOOL GANGSTERS GET AN OLD SCHOOL DEATH.

TIE HIM UP AND TOSS HIM. THAT SHOULD HELP THE KID'S MEMORY.

WAIT... DON'T I GET ANY LAST WORDS?

THOSE WERE THEM.

KICK

NEVER DID *ANYONE* IN THAT WAY. YOU?

NAH. MURDER AIN'T WHAT IT USED TO BE.

MEYER!

THAT WAS A SMART PLAY. I DO KNOW WHERE YOUR COKE IS.

CAPTAIN BASS WAS LYING. IT'S IN THE *LOCKBOX.*

I CAN PICK THE LOCK. NO FUNNY BUSINESS, I PROMISE.

CAN I BORROW A KNIFE?

GUN IS LOADED. DON'T GET SMART.

SNIIKT

I USED TO HAVE MY PIECE OF A GAMING CLUB IN BROWARD COUNTY, THE COLONIAL INN HOTEL.

SOME GUPPY GOT HUNGRY AND STARTED NOSIN' AROUND.

HE SNATCHED UP SOME NEARBY LAND AND OPENED UP HIS OWN CASINO.

HE HAD A GOOD RUN... TURNED A WINNING HAND OR TWO.

SOME MOSERS* FOUND HIM BELLY UP ON HIS SOFA BEFORE I COULD SAY MAZEL AND SEND HIM A CHOCOLATE BABKA.

*COPS

I AM AND ALWAYS HAVE BEEN TOTALLY OPPOSED TO VIOLENCE.

BUT IF YOU GET TOO CLOSE TO SUCCESS...

HUUUUNGH

...DON'T BE SURPRISED WHEN YOU GET A CROWBAR ACROSS THE BACK OF THE HEAD.

THE THING ABOUT PICKING LOCKS...

...THEY'RE ALL BASICALLY THE SAME.

THE ONLY DIFFERENCE...

YOU PULL ANYTHING, YOU JOIN YOUR FRIEND. ¿COMPRENDE?

...IS WHAT'S ON THE OTHER SIDE.

CRAAACK

THWIIIIP

THUNK

CHUKK

YOU SHOW
YOURSELF,
I'LL KILL YOU
QUICK...

CRIK   CRIK

...IF I *FIND* YOU,
I'LL TAKE MY
SWEET TIME.
¿COMPRENDE?

CHARLIE, CHARLIE, CHARLIE... THIS IS THE LOOKOUT BELOW.

CRASH

WHERE'S THE WATER ON THIS TIN CAN?

THERE'S A HOSE ON THE BOW.

KRAK

PLEASE-- I'LL GIVE YOU WHATEVER YOU WANT.

I WANT YOU TO SUFFER.

BLAMM

FZZZT

FSHHHH

GET OUTTA THE WATER, KID!

FZZT
FZZT

ZHAAA ZHAAA

HI—SSSS

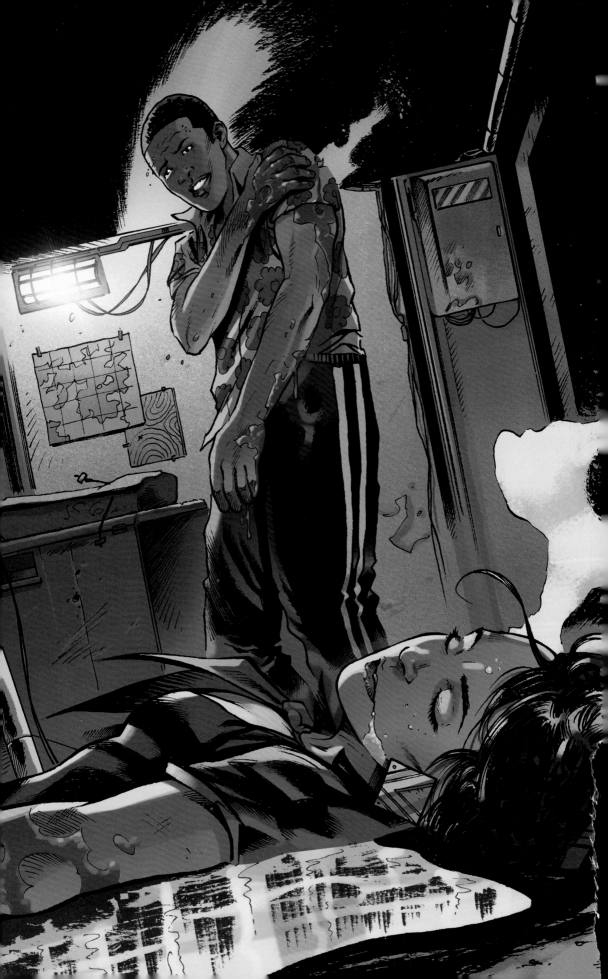

LATER.

IT'S GREAT TO SEE YA, KID. I WAS THINKING ABOUT YOU THE WHOLE WAY UP.

I'M NOT AFRAID TO SAY IT:

NEVER KEEP LOVE UNDER YOUR HAT, KID.

WHERE'S MY MONEY?

SO, UH, DAVID...

YOU NEVER CALL ME DAVID. JUST SPILL IT.

ABOUT THAT BIG PAYDAY OF YOURS... THE HOUSE WON ON THIS ONE. THERE AIN'T ANY KESEV.

MY MISTAKE, I THOUGHT YOU WERE A FRIEND.

I SHOULD'VE NEVER TRUSTED A GODDAMN CRIMINAL.

WHO DO YOU THINK SAVED YOUR TUCHAS? I AM YOUR PAL.

IF MONEY IS MORE IMPORTANT TO YOU THAN YOUR LIFE, THEN YOU HAVEN'T LEARNED A DAMN THING ON THIS CAPER!

IN 1952, RIGHT IN SARATOGA FLORIDA, THEY DID SOMETHING I AIN'T TOO PROUD OF.

THEY THREW THE BOOK AT ME. KEFAUVER PUT ME AWAY AS A COMMON GAMBLER.

THIS WAS THE ONLY TIME IN MY *LIFE* THAT I SPENT TIME IN THE CLINK. I WAS A FISH OUTTA WATER. I WAS A CRIMINAL.

BREAKING IT TO THE KID THAT THIS WHOLE CAPER WAS LITTLE MORE THAN A GRIFT TO GET MY TICKET TO ISRAEL... MAYBE HE WAS RIGHT.

SPLASH

MAYBE I *AM* A *CRIMINAL* AFTER ALL.

I FORGIVE YOU.

YOU AIN'T SORE ABOUT IT?

MEYER, YOU TOLD ME I GOTTA LOOK OUT FOR OTHER PEOPLE, RIGHT?

I GUESS I DID A *MITZVAH*. I GAVE A FRIEND A SECOND CHANCE.

AND ALL THOSE JUDGES OUT THERE, THEY CAN *GET KAKEN AFIN YAM*.* I'M SQUARING IT UP WITH THE ONLY ONE WHO MATTERS.

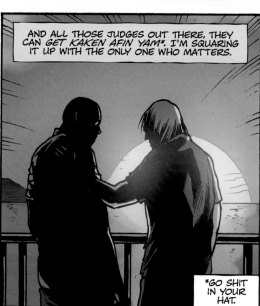

*GO SHIT IN YOUR HAT.

WE *ALL* DESERVE A SECOND-CHANCE, BUT ONLY THE LUCKY ONES GET IT. WAY MORE LUCKY THAN SOME PONIES HITTING A TRI-BOX.

REPEAT AFTER ME... *SHEMA YISRAEL, ADONAI ELOHEINU, ADONAI EKHAD.*

WHAT'S IT MEAN?

IT AIN'T THE MEANING, IT'S THE *FEELING.* WE DODGED A BULLET OR TWO. BE GRATEFUL FOR THAT.

SHEMA YISRAEL, ADONAI ELOHEINU, ADONAI EKHAD.

AS THE SUN BATHES THE WORLD IN PINK--

--YOU BECOME AWARE OF HOW CONNECTED THINGS ARE.

REACTING TO THE SUN IS PRIMAL.

ZZZ

IT'S A FEELING OF HOW TEMPORARY BEAUTY CAN BE.

WHY IT MUST BE HONORED WHEN WE'RE LUCKY ENOUGH TO SEE IT.

SORRY, KID, HERE'S A LITTLE SOMETHING TO MAKE IT UP TO YOU.

THAT *ALMOST* SQUARES US UP.

NOW GO HOME, KID.

THE PINK SUN IS LOVE... THE TREASURE I FOUND IN THE HEART OF ISLAMORADA.

Greetings from the Holy Land, kid.
I picked this up at the Dead Sea.

Went right into the water. Supposed
to be a miracle cure for cuts, so you
never know. It could heal me up nicely.

Starting to actually love the ocean.
Israel is everything I coulda hoped
for. Weather's beautiful, little bit
like Cuba, or Miami.

I know I got more days
behind me than in front,
but I gotta fresh start.
Can't ask for more than
that at my age.

Take care of your mother, your family. They're all that you got.

Everyone deserves a second-chance. Even that no-goodnick dad of yours.

Shalom, kid. If you're ever in the Holy Land, don't forget about your old pal Meyer.

But if anyone comes sniffing around for me...

...keep it under your hat.

Be seeing ya next year in Jerusalem!

MEYER'S YIDDISH MOBSTER GUIDE

Yiddish is a language spoken by the majority of Jews who come from
Eastern Europe. It's German-based with lots of elements borrowed
from Hebrew and Aramaic—the alphabet coming from the latter.
Since the early days of the 20th century, many Jews have come to
America, leaving behind many things—but not their Yiddish!
So, of course, a mobster like Meyer was fully bilingual.
Here are some of the most common words
you'd hear in mob circles...

שאַקרען

SHAKREN (noun) – "A liar. You can't
trust 'em for nothing. Want a tell?
Watch the way his eyes move."

מאַסער

MOSER (noun) – "An informer. The
lowest of the low. Always thinking if
they make a play on their neighbor
they won't get rounded up with the
rest of us. They learned nothin' from
Hitler."

שנאַרער

SCHNORER (noun) – "A cheapskate,
a skinflint. Never go to dinner with
these guys. They order the lobster
and three martinis and they don't
even kick in for tax'n'tip."

האַרט באַכער

HART BOKHER (noun) – "A tough
guy. *See Lucky Luciano.* They'll
take a punch, spit out a tooth and
smile. You want 'em on your side,
but you don't wanna be their
emergency contact."

ANDREA MUTTI'S ORIGINAL DESIGNS

It didn't take MEYER's interior artist, Andrea Mutti, long to come up with great designs for the characters. Here are his original drawings.

Andrea knew exactly how to portray MILENA: beautiful and deadly!

From day one, Andrea was comfortable with the character of MEYER, so the design came instantly.

David, on the other hand, was a bit trickier to grasp. Andrea played around with different fashion and hairstyles to try to capture his essence and attitude.

Last but not least is LEGS FEINSTEIN, who plays a pivotal role in Meyer's journey. He had to look like a stereotypical Jewish business owner in 1980s Florida.

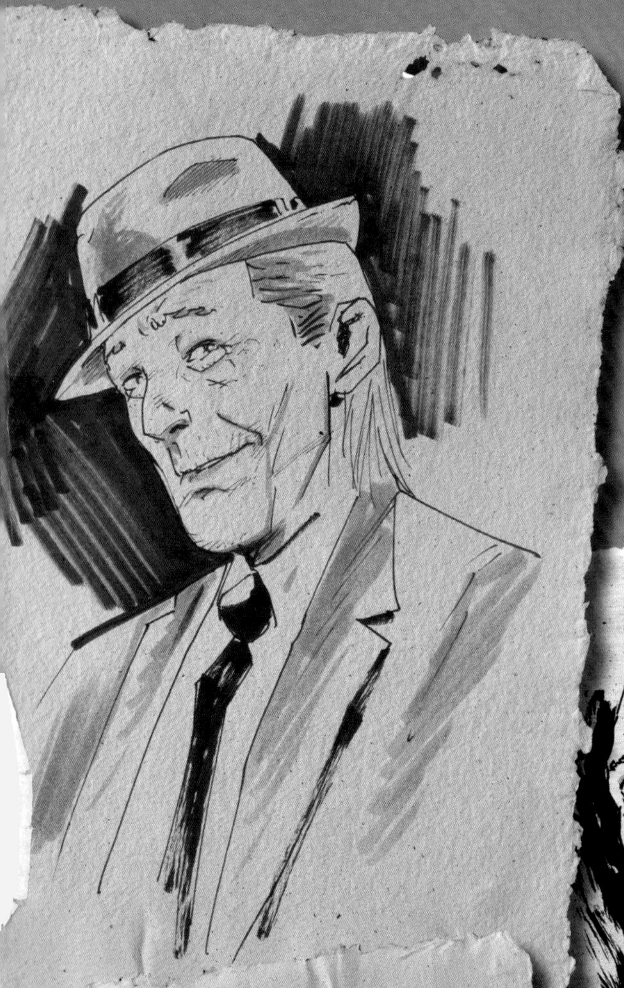

קנאַקקער

KNAKKER (noun) – "A big shot. They only go to synagogue twice a year and buy tickets to sit on the Rabbi's lap. Kinda guy who pulls out a money clip in the middle of 5th Avenue and starts counting."

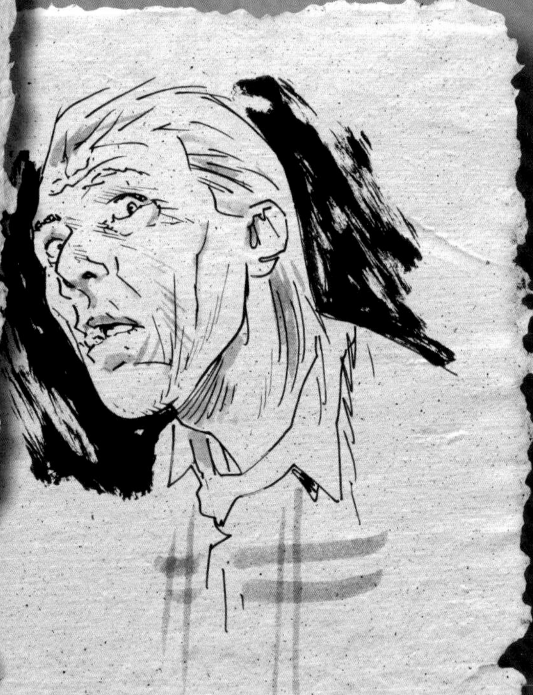

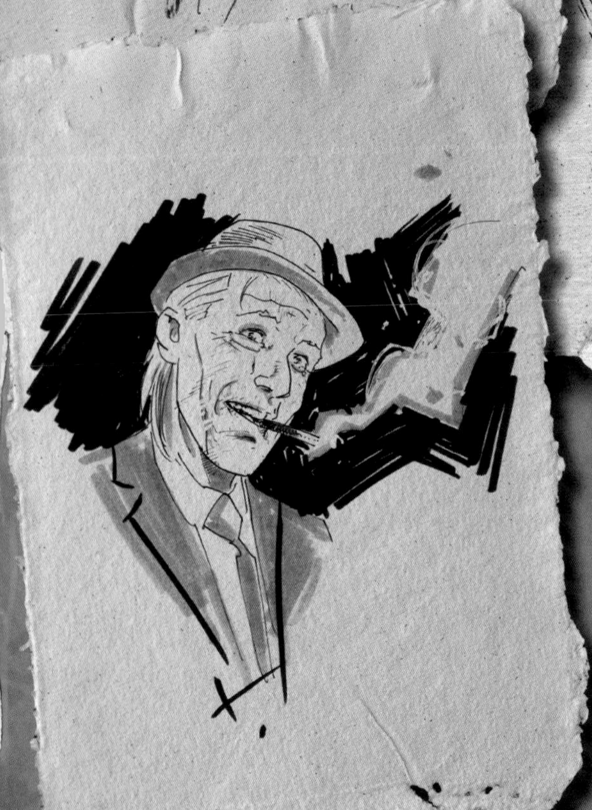

ווייַבערניק

VAYBERNIK (noun) – "A ladies' man. *See Bugsy Siegel*. They look like matinee idols. It isn't just the twinkle in the eye. They know that where they're standing is the place to be."